"Roommates?"

Seth said, sounding skeptical. Jennifer was not like any roommate he'd ever had.

"If you don't mind, I'd like to keep this as informal as possible, Seth. I mean, sure, we'll do our best to stay out of each other's way when necessary, but if we're continually asking permission to come into the room when the door is already wide open, well—" Jennifer was sincerely concerned "—that's going to make life around here very awkward."

"I don't want to make anything uncomfortable for you." Seth sat down on the edge of the bed. "That's the last thing I want, believe me."

Lord, she was adorable right now, he was thinking. What would Jennifer say if he reached out and let his fingers sift through that silky blond hair? What would she say if he leaned over and kissed that sweet mouth of hers again?

This time it wouldn't be in the safety of a crowded restaurant. They were alone. In a bedroom. On a bed . . .

Dear Reader,

Welcome to Silhouette—experience the magic of the wonderful world where two people fall in love. Meet heroines that will make you cheer for their happiness, and heroes (be they the boy next door or a handsome, mysterious stranger) who will win your heart. Silhouette Romance reflects the magic of love—sweeping you away with books that will make you laugh and cry, heartwarming, poignant stories that will move you time and time again.

In the coming months we're publishing romances by many of your all-time favorites, such as Diana Palmer, Brittany Young, Sondra Stanford and Annette Broadrick. Your response to these authors and our other Silhouette Romance authors has served as a touchstone for us, and we're pleased to bring you more books with Silhouette's distinctive medley of charm, wit and—above all—*romance*.

I hope you enjoy this book and the many stories to come. Experience the magic!

Sincerely,

Tara Hughes
Senior Editor
Silhouette Books

VICTORIA GLENN

The Tender Tyrant

Silhouette Romance

Published by Silhouette Books New York

America's Publisher of Contemporary Romance

For my wonderful friend, Lucett,
the original Beverly Hills Blonde

SILHOUETTE BOOKS
300 E. 42nd St., New York, N.Y. 10017

ISBN: 0-373-08628-8

First Silhouette Books printing February 1989

Printed in the U.S.A.

VICTORIA GLENN,

an award-winning writer herself, comes from a family of writers. She makes her home in the Connecticut countryside, but divides her time between the East and West Coasts. She considers it essential to the creative process to visit Disneyland at least twice a year.

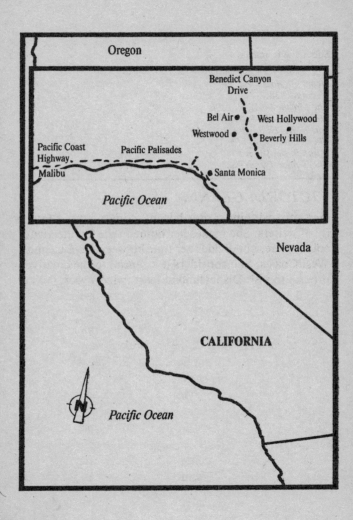

Chapter One

It was a well-known fact that Seth Garrison had ice water in his veins, dollar signs in his eyes and the sense of humor of an artichoke. On the other hand, this was an emergency, and he was the only man Jennifer Ramsey could trust. So she put the proposition before him clearly and concisely, complete with all its legal and financial implications. She was met by an incredulous icy-blue stare.

"You want me to *what*?" he boomed across the desk in utter astonishment.

It was the first time in their twelve-year acquaintance that he had ever raised his voice or revealed more than the slightest flicker of emotion. Jennifer was quite bewildered. "I want you to marry me," she repeated.

"There must be something wrong with the acoustics in my office," Seth Garrison said, slowly removing his glasses. "I thought I heard you make a marriage proposal."

"The acoustics are fine." Jennifer shifted restlessly in the soft leather chair. At first, this had all seemed so simple, so impersonal. Suddenly she wasn't quite sure.

"If this is your idea of a joke, it isn't very funny," came the sharp reply.

"Do you hear me laughing?" Jennifer shook her head. How could she even think of joking at a time like this? Now, of all times, with everything on the line? No, there was far too much at stake. "I've explained to you the circumstances—"

"Indeed you have." He eyed her steadily.

For a moment, she had to struggle for words. "And, well, that is, I admit the situation is somewhat bizarre."

"To say the least."

A strange discomfort began to settle over Jennifer. What had ever led her to believe this task would be easy? But she had no choice. Oliver Ramsey had made quite sure of that. The terms of his will were most specific. No marriage, no inheritance. Everything would then be forfeited to Charlotte, and that was a chilling prospect. "Won't you help me out of this predicament?"

"Why?" There was a peculiar quality to his tone.

She shrugged. "For one thing, the benefits to you financially would be rather substantial."

"I'm well aware of the financial advantages of such an...arrangement." Seth Garrison had an odd expression on his gaunt face. "But you haven't answered my question."

"I've already told you, the document is absolutely incontestable. My lawyers have informed me that failure to comply with the provisions of the bequest will place the bulk of the estate under my stepmother's control."

The man began twisting a steel paper clip intently. "I realize that, but it's still not an answer."

She looked at him curiously. What kind of an answer did he want? "What else could you possibly need to know? I've explained everything. Unless I get married within—"

"I'll be more specific. Why *me*?" His hard fingers continued to ruthlessly bend the tiny wire into a more and more distorted shape. "Of all the men you might have asked, why did you choose me?"

Jennifer was completely nonplussed. "That's a strange question."

"Not at all. It's quite a sensible question." He looked up suddenly. "There are any number of men who meet the conditions of Oliver's will." He turned away to stare out the glass window at the traffic on busy Santa Monica Boulevard, sixteen stories below. "Men who are younger and...far better looking." He paused. "More to your own taste, Jennifer."

It was the first time she could remember him ever calling her by her given name. She cleared her throat with uncharacteristic nervousness. "I don't know what you think I'm looking for, Mr. Garrison. As I've already stated, the marriage would be in name only, to fulfill some idiotic clause in my father's will. This proposition is strictly business."

"But why me?" he probed harshly, turning back to face her. "You could have your pick of practically any man in this town."

In truth, she had never thought of Seth Garrison as a man until this very moment. He had to be thirty-six or thirty-seven by now, yet he appeared almost the same as he had in his twenties. The tortoiseshell glasses, the conservative suit, and even the style of his short brown hair, remained virtually unchanged. Oh, perhaps the cynical line of his mouth seemed etched just a little more deeply these days, and there was a new weariness in his eyes, but for the most part, time had stood still for him. He had been one of her father's most trusted associates and, until recently, a constant presence at the rambling Bel Air estate. Jennifer had known him since she'd been thirteen years old, yet he had never intruded in her life. Although constant, his detached, cool presence had been an unobtrusive one. In the man's own exceedingly quiet and efficient way, he managed to get things done. On the rare occasions when he actually paid any attention to her, it was always with the polite formality of a schoolteacher with a new pupil. "And how are you this morning, Miss Ramsey?'' or ''I trust you enjoyed your Easter vacation, Miss Ramsey.'' Jennifer still couldn't understand Mr. Garrison or exactly what made him tick, but with her present dilemma, every instinct told her that this was the one man she could count on.

''Why me?'' he repeated in a softer tone.

''Because,'' she admitted simply, ''I trust you.''

For a moment there was silence. ''In what way do you trust me?''

''Dad always said you were honest and aboveboard in all your business dealings. I know you wouldn't take advantage of the situation.''

His eyes narrowed unexpectedly. ''Take advantage? In what way wouldn't I take advantage?''

She shrugged. ''There's a good deal of money at stake—''

''I'm not talking about money.''

Jennifer quirked a curious eyebrow. ''Then what *are* you talking about, Mr. Garrison?''

He drew himself up to his full height, which was well over six feet, and slowly walked around to the other side of the desk. Leaning his lanky frame against the polished oak top, he looked down at Jennifer. His silver-blue gaze flickered over her long, sun-streaked hair and down over her soft pink angora dress and rested briefly on her tanned, slender legs. ''What am I talking about indeed, Miss Ramsey?''

Jennifer could not recall an instance when the man had given her more than a rather perfunctory glance before today. It was almost as if she had just caught a glimpse of someone else behind the sedate Seth Garrison she'd known all these years. This strange, new awareness of him made Jennifer uneasy—a curious sensation she chose to ignore. "I haven't the faintest idea."

"If that's really the case, then why did you come here?" he inquired suddenly.

She stared up at him, a subtle plea in her large hazel eyes. "There's nobody else I can ask."

For the slightest instant, a muscle in his jaw tensed. "That's hardly true."

"There's nobody else I *want* to ask," she confessed quietly.

Seth Garrison took a sharp intake of breath. "Jennifer—" He stopped abruptly. "No. My answer is no."

She swallowed her pride and asked again. "Please, change your mind. I need your help."

For a moment there was no reply. Once again his face became hard and unreadable. There was no warmth in his gaze.

This was not what Jennifer had expected—not at all! "I'm in an impossible situation, Mr. Garrison. Won't you reconsider?" she implored.

"No," he uttered harshly. "I can't marry you."

Jennifer was stunned. A blunt refusal was the last thing in the world she had anticipated. Even though she had absolutely no emotional interest in Seth Garrison, the words of his rebuff stung her ears. Inexplicably, tears began to well up in her eyes. "I don't understand—"

"There's obviously quite a lot you don't understand." His tone was sharp.

How could she have been so stupid as to simply assume that he would readily consent to her proposal? But it had seemed so sensible, so logical. Downright practical, in fact. Why would a cool, levelheaded businessman turn down a multimillion-dollar deal? Now Charlotte would win. Charlotte, who was so openly vicious and grasping that she didn't even bother to play the part of the grieving widow. How could something so unthinkable be permitted to happen? "What am I going to do?" she whispered half aloud, fighting back tears of utter frustration. She stared dully at the plush carpet with unseeing eyes. "What am I going to do?" Her voice quavered.

Seth watched the path of a single salty drop as it traveled down her cheek. He compressed his lips tightly and reached into the pocket of his expensive wool suit for a handkerchief. "Oh, damn," he muttered, and pushed the fine linen into her hand.

"Ten million dollars is not an offer to sneeze at," Jennifer said, wiping her eyes miserably.

"I'm not sneezing. Just refusing," Seth replied with unexpected gentleness. "You must realize that my accepting the offer is completely out of the question."

"Why?" she persisted.

"Because your proposition as it stands is unworkable." His gaze rested, unnoticed, on her shiny blond hair. He thought how lovely it was, highlighted by the afternoon sun streaming in through the office window.

Jennifer continued to stare down at the carpet, which was now a beige blur. "I could improve the terms, include stock options, perhaps."

"No thanks." His voice was dry. "I'll pass."

Immediately she raised her head in humiliating realization. "Oh." At last she understood. The thought hadn't even occurred to her before. There had always been enough admiring glances and appreciative remarks from other men, even total strangers. "I'm sorry if the idea of marriage to me is so repugnant, Mr. Garrison."

"Repugnant?" His silver-blue eyes stared at her in disbelief. *"Repugnant?"* He shook his head. "Is that what you think, Jennifer?"

She swallowed miserably. "What else am I supposed to think?" Jennifer reached over to hand back the tear-moistened cloth. The fact that he had used her first name was even more disconcerting than before. "I'm sorry I placed you in such an awkward position."

"For heaven's sake!" Seth took her outstretched hand in his and put the handkerchief back in his jacket pocket. "Wherever did you get such a ridiculous idea?" His grasp was surprisingly warm and firm. Somehow Jennifer had always imagined that this man's touch would be cold.

She was unable to meet his eyes. "Is it really so ridiculous, Mr. Garrison?"

He twisted his mouth. "I'll tell you something that *is* rather ridiculous. Calling me 'Mr. Garrison.'"

"I've always called you 'Mr. Garrison,'" Jennifer murmured. "You've never complained before."

"You never proposed to me before," came the amused reply.

Humor was another characteristic she'd never credited him with. Jennifer shook her head in amazement. "What are you saying?"

"I'm saying that it's about time you started calling me Seth," he said gently. "Incidentally, that's something I should have asked you to do long ago."

"Mr. Garrison, I really don't think—"

"Seth," he prompted.

She sighed. "Seth." The name sounded so strange on her lips. "I meant what I said about putting you in an awkward position." She rose resignedly from the leather chair. "I'm sorry I came here and wasted your time."

"Wait." His hard fingers were still clasping her hand.

"No, really," she insisted brittlely. "I'm sure you have other appointments."

"Would you just hold on for a moment?" he said.

When Jennifer stood up, the movement brought her even closer to where he half sat, half leaned on the edge of his desk. His face hovered scant inches above her own. "I'd better be going."

But his other hand reached out to hold her firmly in place. "Jennifer, what do I have to do to make you stand still?" The hand came to rest firmly on her shoulder.

Through the soft material she could feel a warm, gentle strength. "I guess you're doing it now," she remarked, making an attempt at levity. It was a curious sensation to stand so close to Seth Garrison, to have him touch her in such a—how could one describe it?—an almost proprietary manner. After years of being an aloof, enigmatic stranger, the man seemed almost human.

"Do I make you nervous?" he asked in amazement.

Jennifer shook her head. "Of course not." But that wasn't quite true. He was having a decided effect on her, but it was something indefinable, and she was unable to put a name to it.

"Then why can't you look me straight in the eye, Jennifer?"

There he went again, calling her by her first name. Why did hearing him say it evoke such a curious feeling within her? After all, she had known him nearly half her life, for goodness' sake! "You don't make me nervous," she said stubbornly, still unable to meet his penetrating gaze. *This is supposed to be dull, uninteresting Seth Garrison. Since when has he gone in for penetrating gazes, anyhow?*

"Won't you look at me?" he asked gently.

"I *am* looking at you." Her hazel stare met his blue one reluctantly. There was something in those silvery depths that she was unable to recognize. Something Jennifer had never seen before.

"Do you know why Oliver put that clause in his will?" he asked suddenly.

She lowered her lashes and murmured evasively, "What does that matter now?"

His hands fell to his sides. "Oh, it matters. It matters a great deal." There was a long pause. "Would you care to tell me why he did it?"

Who is the man kidding? Jennifer thought irritably. He must know very well what her father's intentions were all along. At the very least, he must have a vague idea. Until two years ago, Seth Garrison had been Oliver Ramsey's closest confidant. If anyone understood the motivation behind her father's numerous plans and schemes, it would be Mr. Seth Garrison. "I believe you already know why," she replied.

A shadow flickered across his face. "Perhaps you're right," he said in a different tone. "It serves no useful purpose to attempt to second-guess Oliver. Whatever his reasons were, they make little difference at the moment."

Jennifer sensed that this was not the case at all, but what did it matter? Seth Garrison had decided not to press the issue, and for that she was almost grateful. Certain things were simply too personal. Too painful. Even now she could almost hear her father's voice. *How long are you going to keep mourning for Kevin?*

It's unhealthy! Don't make me worry about you, Jenni.

Standing so close to Jennifer, Seth had a strong sense of what she was going through. No one realized how well he understood her loneliness and suffering. No one thought he had even noticed the changes in Oliver's daughter over the years. But he had noticed. He had noticed everything.

He remembered meeting her for the very first time, a smiling child with a huge wad of grape bubble gum in her mouth. She had stood by the exquisitely designed Ramsey swimming pool, disco music blaring from an enormous pastel-colored radio, and regarded him with a mixture of curiosity and disdain. He had grown up surrounded by adults, and he had known virtually nothing about little girls, least of all how to talk to one. It had been a week past his twenty-fourth birthday, and Seth Garrison had felt all the superiority a summa cum laude business-school graduate could possibly muster toward a gum-chewing adolescent.

"How do you do, Miss Ramsey?" He had extended his hand politely. "My name is Seth Garrison, and I've come to work for your father."

Jennifer Ramsey had continued to stare at the gangly man in the serious dark suit. Then, without missing a beat, she had proceeded to blow the most incredibly huge purple bubble the young man had ever seen. Such undignified behavior from the daughter of Oliver Ramsey! Even now, Seth still grinned when he remembered that unbelievable bubble.

He'd pretended to ignore the impudent teenager in the years that had followed, but the truth was that he envied Jennifer Ramsey. She had been adorable, she had been happy, and she had been very much loved by the people around her. Happiness was supposed to be contagious, but it had only made Seth more painfully aware of his own shortcomings. Then, as he had watched his employer's daughter mature into a lovely young woman, a different feeling altogether had replaced his envy. Even now, he wasn't able to put it into words. He didn't even dare permit himself to consider what that feeling was.

He remembered her standing by the swimming pool where he had first met her years before. Only this time she had been dressed in a long blue dress, with a corsage on her wrist. *Senior prom night in Beverly Hills!* The full impact of her beauty had struck Seth with the force of a sledgehammer. Jennifer Ramsey had been a storybook princess posing for the family photographer with her storybook prince. They had both been so young and fresh-faced, their faces radiating anticipation and delight.

He'd wanted to smirk and feel superior. After all, such childish frolics had been beneath the dignity of the very proper Seth Garrison. But in truth he'd felt a strange ache of longing. The emptiness he'd carried around inside had grown even larger and darker. The laughter of the young couple as they posed so happily had splintered into silvery music in the night air. He was still young himself back then, but suddenly the music had made him feel old and alone.

It wasn't until later that the music changed—when the fresh-faced young man of the fairy tale was killed on the highway in Malibu. After that, Jennifer Ramsey, the fairy-tale princess, didn't smile at all. Not for a very long time. And even when she did, it wasn't the same smile he recalled from the night by the swimming pool. It had been almost seven years since Kevin Stern's accident. The fears that Oliver had confided to Seth concerning his daughter had proved well-founded. Seth knew quite well why his old mentor had put such an unorthodox provision in his will. Knowing Oliver, he found such an action almost typical. Yes, there was a stunning, inevitable logic to the situation. The two of them would watch Jennifer in an unguarded moment, as she sat listlessly in the garden or stared into space at the dinner table.

"I've got to do something about my kid," Oliver would say brusquely when the two of them were alone. "I've got to make sure she doesn't end up alone."

Seth would listen silently. What could he do except nod in agreement? But to himself he confessed the worry that nothing even the great Oliver Ramsey could do would cure his daughter's unhappiness. With time, the girl might get over her grief—if she was lucky. He wished there were something he could do, something that would bring the glow of joy back to her young face. Seth Garrison was a realist, however. He knew he was the last person in the world to bring a smile to anyone's face, least of all a young girl's. He knew how to make money, but he knew very little about people. Still, if it had been in his power, he would have given anything to make Jennifer's world whole again.

The woman's quavering voice intruded upon his thoughts. "As I've already said, I apologize for putting you in such an awkward position, Seth."

Shocked back into the present, he stared at her. Jennifer had gathered up her purse and was walking toward the door. "Wait!" he protested with uncharacteristic loudness. "Will you just hold on a minute?" He practically raced across the room.

Jennifer stopped and looked at him in bewilderment. "Yes?"

She called me "Seth," he was thinking. She had called him that without his having to ask her again. It sounded so odd, yet so absolutely right. More important, though, having gotten over the initial shock of her request, he was sure about what he wanted to do next. "About that proposition of yours," he began unsteadily.

Jennifer stood in the doorway, embarrassed. "You've already made it abundantly clear how you feel about that. Why don't we forget I ever came here?"

"Jennifer!" There was an odd vulnerability in his voice.

"What is it?" She hesitated, unsure of what was coming.

Seth cleared his throat. "I've given it some further thought and, upon careful consideration, I would like to accept your proposal."

"You mean you *will*?" Jennifer's hazel eyes widened in happy astonishment.

There was such a poignancy in her relief that he had to force himself to remain unmoved—or at least to pretend to. "As an old friend of your father's, I feel a responsibility to help you in this rather difficult situation," he remarked matter-of-factly.

Jennifer studied him for a long moment. For the life of her, she could not explain the man's sudden about-face. But what did it matter why Seth Garrison had changed his mind? What mattered was that he was going to help her, and that things were going to be all right after all. Her heart practically bubbled over with gratitude. Without thinking, she flung her arms around him in an enthusiastic hug. "Thank you, just thank you! What else can I say?" she declared against his shoulder.

For a moment she felt him stiffen. "It's not necessary to thank me," he said in a strange tone.

She pulled away quickly. "Well, I want to—to thank you, anyway," she stammered. There was an uncomfortable pause. "What happens now?"

With some effort, Seth resumed his old unreadable expression. "The best thing, I suppose, is to have our lawyers meet and discuss the final details." This time, though, *he* was unable to meet her stare. "They can take care of the wedding arrangements, also, unless you would prefer to handle them personally."

The wedding arrangements. It sounded so matter-of-fact, yet somehow it wasn't at all. Maybe in the midst of the shock and confusion of the past few weeks she had begun to imagine things. *My wedding,* Jennifer thought. Years ago she had fantasized and dreamed about what that day would be like. Since losing Kevin, however, she hadn't given such a day another thought. Those happy dreams belonged to some other girl, not to Jennifer Ramsey. She sighed and gazed past Seth Garrison through the floor-to-ceiling office window. Off in the distance she could see the rolling green expanse of the Los Angeles Country Club. "It doesn't matter," she responded sadly. "Let our lawyers arrange everything."

Seth's mouth tightened perceptibly, but he said nothing for a moment. Finally he walked away from her and returned to his desk. "Very well, then," he replied at last, gazing down at the telephone console. "I'll be in touch with you."

Jennifer looked at him in puzzlement. "Thank you again, Seth."

"Forget it," he answered abruptly.

She studied him for a moment, a bewildered expression on her face. Then, with a sigh, she turned

and walked out of the office, shutting the door behind her.

Seth Garrison slowly looked up from his desk. He
stared at the closed door for a long time.

Chapter Two

Until two years ago, Jennifer had considered the sprawling Tudor-style mansion in the hills above Sunset Boulevard her home. More than a home, actually. Those seven tranquil, tree-covered acres had encircled not only the house she had grown up in but much more. The house had been a serene fortress, a gentle barrier against everything unpleasant in the world. It was only a five-minute drive to the nearby campus of the University of California in Westwood, and the trip had been the pattern of her life since her graduation from high school. Her life had alternated between school and home, and she had seldom gone anywhere else.

At first her father had seemed delighted at her proximity. It had been reassuring for a man so rich

and powerful to know that his only child was almost
always within sight, safe and sound. After all, the
world could be a dangerous and unpredictable place,
especially for the daughter of the celebrated Oliver
Ramsey III. He was a man accustomed to the risks
that too often accompanied fame and success. Starting with a huge inheritance derived from the vast
Ramsey publishing empire, Oliver had expanded to
even greater things, applying his characteristic golden
touch. Now the empire ranged from the controlling
interest in a motion-picture studio to substantial
holdings in computer software, frozen food and even
a domestic airline. But one particular acquisition made
by the multimillionaire had been not only impractical
but extremely unsettling. At the age of sixty-five,
Oliver Ramsey had acquired a new wife. And his
choice had been every bit as unpredictable and astonishing as Mr. Ramsey himself—Charlotte DeLeon, a
film actress nearly thirty years his junior. They had
married just as Jennifer had entered graduate school.

Even now, as she drove home, fresh from her encounter with Seth Garrison, Jennifer recalled the bit-
terness of those first few weeks after the new Mrs.
Ramsey had arrived on the scene and begun trans-
forming her once-peaceful retreat into a battle-
ground. Charlotte DeLeon was beautiful and
charming, to be sure, but her beauty was only on the
surface. As for the charm, that quickly evaporated in
the presence of people who didn't matter to Charlotte. She considered her stepdaughter one of those

people. The two women had never tried to conceal their mutual dislike. Within a month Jennifer had moved out of her beloved home and into an apartment. Not long after that, Jennifer recalled, Seth Garrison had left his position as her father's right-hand man and started his own corporation in Beverly Hills. Whether the two men had had some kind of falling out or had simply parted friends, she had no idea. The one thing she *did* know was that before today, the only time she had seen Seth Garrison in the past two years had been at her father's funeral.

Jennifer turned down a quiet avenue lined with palm trees, pausing in front of a four-story stucco building. She pressed the automatic garage door opener, which was kept clipped to the sun visor, and waited for the metal grate to lift up. In another moment Jennifer pulled into the subterranean parking area.

In the dusky silence of the empty garage, she sat pensively for some time. There was no hurry. She had nowhere to go. She had no reason to do anything but simply sit in her car in the semidarkness and think. This past month had been the worst of her life. Jennifer would not have believed that she could ever again feel such a gut-wrenching loss as she had experienced when Kevin had been killed. Now she knew how wrong she had been. Here again was the bitter denial followed by raw pain and then the inevitable numbness.

Finally, with great reluctance, Jennifer emerged from her automobile and headed wearily toward the lobby entrance. Once upstairs in her comfortable apartment with its soothing hues of lavender and beige, she turned on the stereo and tried not to think about anything. But peace still eluded her. The week before her father's death, Jennifer had handed in her master's thesis in early American literature. Until then, research and study had occupied her time and thoughts. But now there was nothing to distract her from the harsh realities of her situation. Oliver Ramsey, the one loving anchor in her life, was gone, and he had left a disturbing legacy. She grimaced in disgust, recalling the stunned expression on Charlotte's beautiful, thin face as the two of them had sat in the lawyer's office watching a videotaped reading of Oliver's will.

"Is he crazy?" the older woman had hissed at the television screen when her late husband had revealed the unorthodox conditions of his bequest. "Does he really expect me to settle for a few lousy million while you get everything else?" Then Charlotte had turned her attention to Jennifer. "Do you really think I'm that stupid, Little Miss Princess?"

It had been a shocking and extremely bitter scene. Even Oliver's attorneys had seemed taken aback by Charlotte's vicious tirade. What would her stepmother say when she heard the news of Jennifer's impending marriage? Jennifer twisted her mouth wryly and went into her small kitchen to pour herself a diet cola.

Charlotte would be apoplectic with rage, but the truth was, Jennifer didn't care. She had more difficult problems to confront now. As she leaned against the breakfast bar, the staggering impact of her confrontation with Seth Garrison finally hit her.

I'm marrying a man I scarcely know in just a few days' time!

It was a little terrifying to think about the situation. *Let our lawyers arrange everything.* Wasn't that what she had told Seth Garrison? There would be piles of legal documents to be signed, that was for sure, followed by a brief and hopefully quiet wedding ceremony. Jennifer prayed there wouldn't be any prying questions about the hasty marriage. That was the last intrusion she was in the mood to tolerate. It was bad enough to consider the changes in privacy that marriage might bring. It occurred to Jennifer that she might have to change her current residence. No, she thought, quickly shaking her head. No one, not even the lawyers, would expect her to give up her privacy in such a radical way. She took another sip of cola. But even in a name-only marriage, it was perfectly reasonable that she might be expected to play the role of the devoted wife, particularly in a place such as Beverly Hills. Seth Garrison was a prominent businessman, and Jennifer saw that she might have no choice but to assume many social responsibilities.

Well, she thought, sighing resignedly and setting her plastic tumbler on the counter, an occasional appearance at a charity function or a business dinner probably wouldn't kill her. Still, it was hard to believe she was actually going to become Mrs. Seth Garrison, even if it would only be on paper. The entire situation was ludicrous. Poor Oliver had meant well, she knew, but the situation he had forced on Jennifer was absurd. Old-fashioned in his outlook, her father had sincerely believed that a woman could not find happiness until she settled down with a husband and a family.

Seth Garrison. On top of all the other recent surprises, his behavior had been the most astonishing of all. The man had actually shown a degree of warmth. Of course, it might all be her imagination working overtime. After so many years, a leopard didn't suddenly change his spots, did he?

Her reverie was interrupted by the telephone ringing.

"Jennifer..." said a familiar deep voice.

"Oh, Mr. Garrison." *Speak of the devil!*

"It's Seth, or do we have to go through that again?" he said impatiently.

"Seth," Jennifer said hastily, still ill at ease with this new informality. It seemed more awkward speaking with him on the telephone than it had been face-to-face. Those brief moments of warmth in his office might just as well never have happened. How strange that with all her social skills Jennifer could still feel so uncomfortable in the presence of a man she had known nearly half her life. Now that she was going to marry him, she had best stop thinking of him as Mr.

Garrison—even if it was only going to be a paper marriage.

"I'd like to get together with you this evening," Seth began evenly.

"Why?"

"What do you mean, why?" There was a slight edge to his voice. "Does there have to be a reason?"

Fear gripped Jennifer. "Are you trying to tell me you've changed your mind?"

"About what?"

"You know very well what. Is this your way of letting me know that you've had time to reconsider the situation and you don't want to go through with it after all?"

"Is that what you think?"

"Well, *have* you?" Jennifer's tension was evident in her voice.

There was an audible pause. "Would it really bother you if I had?"

"That's not an answer."

"It wasn't much of a question," he retorted. "Of course I haven't changed my mind. Don't be ridiculous, Jennifer."

There was an uneasy silence. "All right." She sighed. "Let's start all over again. Did you say you wanted to get together tonight?"

"That was the general idea, yes."

"To talk about this . . . this thing, I suppose."

He seemed taken aback. "This *thing*, as you call it, is a wedding. I realize it's just a legal arrangement, but you needn't sound so cold-blooded about it."

His chastening tone astonished her. It was rather embarrassing to be called cold-blooded by Seth Garrison, of all people. "Would you prefer it if I were dreamily sentimental or maudlin?" she shot back defensively.

"Certainly not," came the brittle reply. "I would never want you to make any pretense about your feelings or lack of them. Just be yourself." He hesitated. "If you really want to know the truth, I half expected *you* to change your mind about all this."

"Me?" Jennifer was caught off guard. "Now who's being ridiculous, Seth? Why on earth would I want to change my mind?"

"There are other men you might have asked," he told her in a strange voice. "I figured when you had time to think about it—"

Jennifer interrupted him, her tone guarded. "Wait a minute. Is this your tactful way of backing out? Because if you regret having made such a hasty decision, I understand. I mean, what if you have a girlfriend? I never even considered that." Oh, Lord, how could she have been so stupid? It had never even occurred to her—

"Would you just be quiet for a minute, Jennifer?" Seth sounded exasperated. "For the hundredth time, I haven't changed my mind. And as for the other thing, do you honestly believe I would have consented to marry you, even in name only, if I were currently involved with another woman? What kind of person do you think I am?''

"It's just that I assumed—''

"Stop assuming, Jennifer Ramsey. It's that easy.'' His tone became kinder. "Now, would you allow me to get to the point of this phone call? There are certain things I'd prefer to discuss with you in person.''

"Such as?''

"I've just gotten a call from my lawyer.''

"Oh.'' There was the oddest sensation in Jennifer's stomach.

"Apparently he and your own attorneys have already set the wheels in motion.'' He cleared his throat. "In any event, I'd rather talk to you about this in person if you happen to be free this evening.''

"Of course I'm free,'' she answered hastily. "What would I be doing?''

"I thought you might have a date,'' Seth offered bluntly.

"Now who's making assumptions?'' Jennifer accused. "What kind of person do you think *I* am, Seth Garrison?''

For a moment the man on the other end of the line seemed nonplussed. Then he gave a short laugh. "Touché.''

They agreed to go out for dinner. Seth suggested a quiet place both of them knew and said he would come by Jennifer's apartment at eight-thirty to pick her up.

She wasn't quite sure what to wear to meet him. It wasn't a date, but it wasn't exactly a business meeting, either. Jennifer wanted to keep the mood casual without appearing too informal. In the end she settled for a short gray wool skirt and a white turtleneck sweater. She slipped on a matching pair of gray suede boots and pulled her long hair back into a ponytail. Examining her silver pendant watch, a treasured childhood Christmas gift, Jennifer noted that the time was 8:29. She smiled. Everything she could recall about Seth Garrison convinced her that the man would be absolutely punctual. Not a minute early, and not a minute late.

Jennifer had a moment to reflect upon the situation. She admitted she felt a little shy around Seth Garrison, but that alone was not responsible for her reticence tonight. It had been a long time since she'd gone out, except for an occasional movie with friends. Going out with acquaintances for drinks or dinner were activities Jennifer hadn't particularly relished lately. Her father had gone so far as to comment that she was well on her way to becoming a social recluse. The truth was that it was difficult for Jennifer to find many people who were only interested in her friendship. Often, when people found out who her father was, they wanted to wangle an introduction to the man. Jennifer sighed. Growing up in Beverly Hills, the children of the affluent and powerful usually adopted one of two styles of behavior. They would either go for the flash or make themselves as unobtrusive as possible. Depending on one's inner confidence, either strategy could be quite successful. Jennifer herself had gone through both phases and had ultimately wound up somewhere in the middle.

She shrugged, adjusting the collar of her knit top. Actually, it might be a relief to spend some time in Seth's company. He served as a reminder of happier days, before Oliver had married Charlotte. No one else had known Oliver as well as Jennifer had, except for Seth. Unexpectedly a tear trickled down her cheek. Well, if it was any consolation, at least she was following her father's last wishes. And Jennifer had long suspected that he had considered Seth Garrison a most suitable candidate for the position of son-in-law. Even though this was just going to be a brief marriage of convenience, she couldn't help but admit that with this strange turn of events Oliver Ramsey was getting his own way after all.

As if on cue, the intercom buzzed. It was precisely 8:30. Despite her bittersweet thoughts, Jennifer couldn't keep a slight smile from crossing her lips. She pressed the receiver button. The familiar voice could be heard through the crackling transmission. Moments later, Seth appeared in the doorway. Still dressed in the same three-piece suit, he looked just as crisp and neat as he had earlier in the day. Jennifer wondered if the man ever wrinkled his clothing like other human beings.

He just stood there for a minute, regarding her quietly. "Hello, Jennifer." His appraisal of the gently clinging sweater and short skirt was brief but thorough. "You look very—"

"Presentable?" she interrupted hopefully.

He paused. "*Pretty* was actually the word I had in mind."

"Oh." A slight flush suffused Jennifer's skin. She was not used to compliments from Seth Garrison. Since this afternoon she had been forced to look at him in a completely different way. As he took a step into the hallway, she was aware that something in the atmosphere had subtly altered.

"You have a lovely apartment." Seth surveyed the soft color scheme, the cotton print sofa and throw cushions and the natural wood furniture. Numerous museum posters adorned the walls. He adjusted his glasses, gazing over at one of the prints. "I saw that Van Gogh exhibit in New York a while ago."

"I heard it was wonderful."

Seth nodded. "All the paintings were done during the last year of his life—less than a year, really. Just a few brief months, yet he poured every bit of talent and emotion onto those canvases. You could see the sequence of his moods and feel the way he felt with the days slipping through his fingers—" He stopped himself, embarrassed. "I didn't mean to bore you, rattling on like that."

"It wasn't boring," Jennifer insisted. "I had no idea you were interested in art." *No idea at all.* It was positively enlightening to hear Seth Garrison get excited about a subject other than high finance.

"Does it surprise you that much, Jennifer?" he inquired softly.

"Well..." She hesitated.

"I'm willing to bet that there are quite a few things about me that would surprise you." Seth studied her face, his expression unreadable. "Shall we go to dinner?"

Marcello's was an unpretentious but expensive restaurant nestled on the outer fringes of Beverly Hills. The lighting was dim enough to ensure both atmosphere and privacy. Unlike so many of the newer, trendier dining spots, with their sleek, high-tech decor and incredibly high noise levels, Marcello's belonged to a more traditional Los Angeles. It featured dark carpeting, comfortable leather banquettes and rich wood paneling that had mellowed with age. There was no tinny rock music to drown out quiet conversation, no constant clatter of tableware being plunked on nearby tables by frenzied waiters. Everything was muted and soothing. Jennifer felt relaxed the moment they took their seats.

Seth waited until she had started on her glass of wine and then began talking slowly. "There's a friend of mine named Harold Helmer. He's a superior court judge downtown, and—"

She set her glass down and glanced at him curiously. "And?"

He eyed her steadily. "He's agreed to perform the ceremony on Sunday afternoon."

For a moment the room swam in front of her. "*This* Sunday?"

"That's correct." There was a long silence. "Is that a satisfactory arrangement for you, Jennifer?"

"Y-yes, of course," she stammered at last, practically choking on her chardonnay. "It just all seems to be happening so fast."

"You *did* impress upon me that time was of the essence," Seth reminded her coolly.

"I know, but—"

"And apparently Oliver's lawyers feel quite strongly about it," he continued. "They've informed my attorney that Charlotte has initiated some tricky legal maneuvering. The sooner you can fulfill the conditions of the will, the more likely it is they'll be able to head off any monkey wrench she might throw into the works."

"I see." Jennifer met his probing stare. "So we'll get married Sunday..." She gripped the stem of her wineglass unconsciously. "That's . . . fine."

"It's my turn to ask you." Seth reached across the table and gently touched her clenched fingers. "Are you having second thoughts about this?"

"Of course not!" she said hotly. "Why would you think that?"

His silver-blue gaze did not waver. "Because I know that this little 'detour' is not quite what you had in mind for your life right now."

Jennifer was disturbingly aware of the quiet strength of his grasp. "I'm sure that this isn't exactly what *you* had planned for your social agenda, either."

"You sound very sure about that."

"Of course I'm sure," she countered. "To be quite frank, you never impressed me as the marrying type."

Seth released her fingers. "That's fascinating. I can see there are several misconceptions about me that I'll have to dispel."

"Are you saying I'm wrong?"

He quirked an eyebrow. "What makes you believe that I wouldn't be interested in a permanent relationship with—" he hesitated "—the right woman?"

Jennifer smiled vaguely. "Well, there you are. The right woman. According to most men, that so-called paragon never seems to come along."

"Is that so?"

She gave a shrug. "Sure. Just take a look at the statistics. Millions of bright, attractive women, and not enough males to go around."

"I disagree."

"How can you argue with facts?" Jennifer insisted. "Have you any idea how difficult it is for so many women I know? They simply can't find any men these days."

Seth twisted his mouth. "Maybe they're looking in the wrong places."

"I doubt it."

"Or perhaps most women don't recognize the right man when they see him. Their ideal mate might be right under their noses all the time, but they don't realize it.'' He poured himself some more wine from the bottle chilling in the cooler. ''This town is a perfect example of how people—most people—prefer flash over substance.''

Jennifer leaned back against the banquette. ''If you're talking about most women, I'd say you're wrong, Seth Garrison.''

''Am I?'' He set his wineglass on the table so forcefully that the golden liquid splashed up against the rim. ''Let me tell you from personal experience, I happen to be one hundred percent right. In fact, I've made a study of this phenomenon.''

''Really?''

''Really.''

''Would you care to be more specific and illustrate your point with a few examples?'' Maybe it was the wine, or perhaps the easy repartee had led her down a careless path. Now Jennifer realized from the sudden silence that her question had been a rather insensitive one. ''I shouldn't have asked you that. I'm sorry.''

''Don't be ridiculous, Jennifer. Your question was a perfectly valid one. I'm merely at a loss as to how exactly to . . . answer it.'' Something odd glinted in his eyes. ''What I might start with saying is—''

''Hey, Jenni!'' a familiar female voice suddenly called out.

Jennifer looked up with a smile. ''Anita?''

''C'est moi!'' responded the stunning redhead approaching their table. Anita Bailey was Hollywood's latest rising star, but to Jennifer she was still the plump little nine-year-old who had desired only to be an airline stewardess. The two of them had been best friends since they'd attended the same exclusive private school in nearby Brentwood. As shy first-graders, they had been inseparable once paired off together in the size-place line.

"You look terrific," Jennifer told her friend, "but then you always do." The other woman looked as if she had been poured into her violet tube dress. Her vivid hair was perfect, and she wore aquamarines and pearls everywhere.

"Are you kidding?" Anita grinned. "I look like a Fabergé Easter egg." She glanced curiously at Seth. "Mr. Garrison? Gee, I haven't seen you in ages!"

Seth gave a resigned smile. "What kind of epidemic is this, anyhow? Does every human being under the age of thirty feel compelled to call me by my last name?"

Anita shrugged. "You'll always be 'Mr. Garrison' to me. I can't believe you even have a first name."

"It's Seth," Jennifer informed her quickly.

Anita looked back and forth between the two of them tentatively. "Well, I hope you still aren't mad at Jenni and me for tossing all those water balloons at you."

Jennifer turned a bright crimson. "Why did you have to bring that up?" They had been thirteen years old at the time, and the pompous young man standing in the courtyard below had represented a tempting target from Jennifer's bedroom window. The sight of Seth Garrison dripping wet in his drab suit and tie was something she had never forgotten. Gracious, even his glasses had looked waterlogged.

"I guess you'd say I'm the forgiving type," Seth remarked now.

"Then there was that time we spilled nail polish on your car," Anita reflected nostalgically.

"That was an accident!" Jennifer protested.

"I forgot that long ago," Seth assured her.

"Boy, were we awful kids!" Anita declared.

"The worst," Jennifer confessed.

"Youthful high spirits," Seth told them. "I hope you two haven't lost any sleep over it."

Jennifer could hear the laughter in his tone. In truth, she was embarrassed, recalling all those childish pranks at Seth's expense. How strange that he had borne it all stoically, never once complaining to Oliver Ramsey about her mischievous behavior. During the infamous water-balloon incident he'd just stood there, wiping off his glasses with a handkerchief. He'd merely shaken his head disapprovingly, the water still dripping from his drenched hair in rivulets, and stared up at the two giggling schoolgirls for a brief moment.

"Very mature," he'd muttered curtly, and then he'd walked away.

It was hard to believe that years later they could all sit around and joke about it. Back then she hadn't thought Seth Garrison was capable of laughing at anything. Perhaps that was why she had always played pranks on him, trying to provoke a reaction. To her eternal irritation, he had never risen to the bait. How that had gotten under her skin!

"So," Anita was asking now, "it's been days since I last saw you, kid. Anything new?"

"No, nothing." Jennifer glanced at Seth, who sat watching her silently.

"Tell me about it. Always the same old grind." She tossed back her long red mane. "At least you're getting out again. Honestly, Mr. Garri—I mean Seth—sometimes I have to practically hold a gun to Jenni's head to get her to even go to a movie!"

"Oh?" He seemed genuinely surprised.

Anita gazed in the direction of the bar, where a handsome young television actor was talking urgently into a telephone receiver. "I know what you're going to say, Jenni." She sighed. "I really ought to stop dating a guy who's carrying on a love affair with his answering machine."

"Did I say a single word?"

"Nah, but I could always read your mind, Jennifer Ramsey. Haven't we known each other since we were six years old?"

"Don't remind me!" Jennifer groaned.

Just then, the man at the bar hung up the phone and looked questioningly toward Anita. "Well, I'd better go," she said. "Otherwise Rod is going to come over here and bore you guys to death." She waved goodbye to both of them. "Nice to see you after two hundred years." The young actress grinned at Seth, who gave her a friendly nod. "And *you* better call me tomorrow," she commanded Jennifer. "I have tons of gossip for you!"

"I'll wait with bated breath," Jennifer said, dismissing her genially.

They both watched Anita stride away toward the bar. There was a long pause. "Is there a reason why you didn't mention our impending marriage to Anita?" Seth finally inquired, an almost chiding quality in his tone.

She lowered her eyes evasively. "I didn't think it was necessary."

He seemed taken aback. "She's your best friend, isn't she?"

"Yes, but—"

"But what?" Seth's jaw tensed. "Are you ashamed to introduce me as your fiancé?"

"Of course not!" Jennifer looked up at him in utter amazement. "Where did you get such a ridiculous idea, Seth?"

He looked down at the table, suddenly aware that he had mindlessly crushed several breadsticks. What had gotten into him all of a sudden, anyhow? Since when had he become such a supersensitive moron? Hadn't he agreed to go along in this charade knowing full well that Jennifer Ramsey wasn't even in his league? How could he blame her for feeling understandably embarrassed and awkward about the situation? When she had come to his office this afternoon with her staggering proposal, Seth had realized that a golden opportunity had fallen into his lap. This was the woman who had always obsessed him, the woman he had always believed was out of reach. It had been a revelation when Jennifer had informed him that *he* was the one man she could turn to . . . the one man she could trust. Sure, he knew she probably didn't care about him in more than a friendly way, but that was a start.

Seth studied his young dinner companion. She looked so beautiful with those hazel eyes and that silky hair. So many times he'd wanted to reach out and touch her hair but known he dared not. How close he'd come to making a total fool of himself earlier. Like some adolescent schoolboy, he had almost revealed his feelings for Jennifer. Fortunately, they had been interrupted at that precise moment by Anita Bailey. *That was a close call,* Seth thought, chastising himself. Jennifer Ramsey was still emotionally fragile. She had never gotten over the loss of her high-school sweetheart, and there was nothing more difficult than competing with a ghost. Seth couldn't afford to be careless with the force of his own emotions. Jennifer would have to be wooed gently. Slowly. Besides, she already trusted him. Depended upon him. Who could say what might happen once they were actually married?

"Seth?" Jennifer stared at him in puzzlement. "If I've done anything to offend you, I'm very sorry. It's just that I'd rather tell Anita about the engagement tomorrow." She glanced around the room. "Her voice really carries, and the last thing we want is an audience.''

Seth assumed his blandest smile. ''Goodness, Jennifer. Can't you tell when a person is just teasing you?'' He was gratified to see the relief in those hazel eyes.

''Then you understand what I mean?''

''I understand *perfectly*,'' Seth assured her, just the right note of casualness in his tone.

Chapter Three

Once Anita Bailey swept into the night with her escort, the evening became considerably more tranquil. If there had been any tension or awkwardness earlier, it seemed to have evaporated. Seth went out of his way to make Jennifer feel at ease. Over tortellini and veal piccata, he regaled her with delightful anecdotes about Oliver. For the first time in weeks, Jennifer could feel some of the numbness starting to recede. Just to be able to hear someone else who remembered her father as a unique, vibrant human being meant everything now that he was gone.

"I always wondered why you quit working for Ramsey Enterprises," she asked Seth.

He shrugged. "It's a long story. Why don't we just say that it was time to strike out on my own?"

"And you're doing quite well at it, too, I understand."

"Oh, I get by," he agreed modestly.

Jennifer suppressed a smile. Seth Garrison had never been one to blow his own horn. The fact was that in less than two years the man had become one of the most successful investment advisers in Los Angeles.

But talking about himself didn't interest Seth. "Tell me about your master's thesis," he asked. "Oliver was very proud of your academic achievements."

Jennifer sipped her cappuccino. "I really shouldn't bore you."

He arched an eyebrow. "Why would it bore me?"

"Not too many people these days get excited about Washington Irving."

"Nonsense," he smiled back. "I'm a Rip Van Winkle fan from way back."

For the next hour she told Seth all about her paper on the man Jennifer had long considered the greatest American writer. "I realize most people don't agree with me. They call me old-fashioned and challenge me with Twain and Hemingway."

"Well, literature, like all art, is a pretty subjective thing." He leaned back against the leather banquette. "As far as I'm concerned, life would be exceedingly dull if everyone had the same tastes."

"I agree. Imagine what the world would be like if everybody loved the same music, the same food—"

"The same people?" Seth interjected softly.

Jennifer was somewhat bewildered by the subtle shift in their conversation. Was it her imagination, or was there a hint of sensuality in Seth's words? "The first two conditions would make life rather dull. The one you mention would make life a disaster," she declared matter-of-factly.

"To say the very least."

Then again, thought Jennifer, when was the last time she had given much thought to the concept of love? It was not an emotion that had particularly concerned her in the past few years. She assumed a casual tone. "Of course, I don't consider myself much of an authority. How about you? Would you call yourself an authority on the highly touted subject of love?"

"No." His answer was astonishingly abrupt. He glanced at his watch. "I had no idea it was this late. We both have early starts tomorrow."

Was it late? Jennifer realized it was nearly eleven o'clock. The evening had gone by so fast that she hadn't checked her own watch once. The obvious answer was that Seth Garrison, a man she had always considered stiff and uninteresting, had proved to be a most entertaining dinner companion.

During the ride home, Seth was strangely untalkative. Jennifer took advantage of the silence to observe his taut profile. It had never occurred to her before that he was a rather attractive man. Certainly not until today. The type of looks she had always preferred had been classic, all-American features—such as Kevin's. Blond, husky, always smiling. Like a surfing football player, she had often told him teasingly. But the man driving her home in his Mercedes sedan tonight had a completely different kind of appeal. He was not handsome in the conventional sense, yet his tanned, angular features were nonetheless arresting. Though he seldom smiled, she knew now that he was quite capable of humor. Studying the determined set of his mouth, she wondered what those lips would feel like against her own.

Jennifer inwardly chastised herself. Gracious, what was the matter with her? Why was she suddenly having such absurd thoughts about Seth—thoughts that, if she were to be completely honest, almost verged on the erotic? Rarely in the past few years had she permitted herself to indulge in such thoughts. In truth, her senses had become dulled after the loss of Kevin, but whenever a stray fantasy surfaced, Jennifer had always pushed it from her mind. Until recently, it had seemed wrong, disloyal somehow, to think about any man but her late fiancé. If she did entertain such thoughts, it would mean Kevin was truly gone forever. It panicked her to sense the cherished memory of a loved one slowly fading from her life.

The car drew up to an empty space in front of Jennifer's apartment complex, and Seth turned off the engine. In the dim light, he faced her. "I know this situation is rather awkward for both of us, but I—" He stopped for a moment, searching for the right words. "I want to reassure you that everything is going to work out. We're going to carry it off, Jennifer. You'll receive what's rightfully yours from Oliver, and you'll be happy."

Jennifer shrugged. "That remains to be seen."

"Trust me on this. You will *not* be cheated out of your inheritance by anyone, least of all that loathsome woman."

She was amazed at the acid in his tone when he referred to Charlotte. "Well, if we do beat her, I'll have you to thank. There's no way I'd be able to pull this off without you, Seth." Jennifer was absolutely sincere in her gratitude. "You'll have really earned that ten million, believe me."

A muscle in his jaw tensed. "Forget about the money."

"I beg your pardon?"

"I'm not doing it for the money. I never said anything about the money, did I?"

Jennifer stared up at him. "Of course you did, this afternoon.... I don't understand!"

"I merely said I was accepting your proposal."

"Right. You agreed to specific terms of financial remuneration," Jennifer insisted, growing more and more bewildered by the minute.

"Let me make this very clear," Seth said. "I am doing this because I want to help you out of an impossible situation. Oliver had the best intentions, but he went too far. It was wrong to put you in such a position. He was foolish to gamble with his child's legacy." Seth was using the same authoritative tone that intimidated the captains of industry. "Understand me, Jennifer. I owe it to the friendship I had with your father all these years to make sure everything ends happily for you."

Could this really be Seth Garrison speaking? The man she had once accused of having an adding machine for a heart? "But the ten million dollars—"

"If you mention ten million dollars again, the wedding is off. You can go over to Disneyland and shanghai one of the seven dwarfs. Might I suggest either Bashful or Grumpy?"

Jennifer managed a thin smile. "Why would you do this, Seth?" It was still difficult to believe the man had no intention of accepting money that was so freely offered.

"I don't want to dwell on this. Suffice it to say I would find it personally offensive to see the daughter of Oliver Ramsey cheated out of her birthright. If there's one thing I detest, it's an injustice."

Today was turning out to be one surprise after another—all in the person of Seth Garrison. Jennifer had no doubt that the man was being honest. He meant what he was saying. It all seemed so incredibly noble and unselfish. *And completely unreal.* "I don't know what to say," she finally managed to murmur.

"Don't say anything." Seth reached into his jacket and pulled out a small box. "By the way, I meant to give you this at the restaurant, but when you made that comment about not wanting an audience I realized you were right."

She looked at the small package questioningly. "What is it?"

"Something you'll need if we intend to convince the population of Beverly Hills that we are legitimately engaged." He slid apart the silver wrapping and removed a velvet-covered jeweler's box. "Give me your left hand, Jennifer," came the gentle command.

"What are you do—"

In another moment Seth slid an exquisitely made diamond ring onto her third finger. "That's better," he declared with satisfaction. "*Now* you look the part."

The marquise-cut diamond had to be at least four carats. "This really isn't necessary," she argued hopelessly. Seth was right. Of course he was right. Who in their circle of acquaintances, particularly Charlotte, would believe that a marriage was legitimate without such a glittering prop?

"It becomes you," Seth murmured softly.

She continued to stare at the sparkling bauble. "This is quite beautiful, but you must have spent a fortune."

"I'm just pleased that you like it."

"Who wouldn't? Of course, be sure and keep the receipt so I can reimburse you for the expense," Jennifer said genially.

"That isn't necessary." There was a tone of reproof in his response.

"Oh, don't be absurd. I insist," Jennifer said earnestly. "Why should you undertake any expense at all in this situation?"

"I don't want to argue about it." Seth's mouth was set in a hard line. "Just wear the ring."

Jennifer knew an outrageously expensive piece of jewelry when she saw one. What she couldn't understand was why this man seemed so adamant about paying for the item out of his own pocket. Under the circumstances, Seth's attitude made no sense. "You're being ridiculous."

"And you're stubborn."

"*I'm* stubborn?"

"Let's not spend the entire night debating about some little trinket."

"I would hardly call this a trinket." Jennifer was actually embarrassed. The value of the gem was unmistakable.

"Call it anything you wish."

"Listen here, Seth Garrison." She leaned toward the driver's seat to make her point. "If you don't allow me to pay for this ring, I swear I'll toss it right back at you!"

His eyes glinted in the moonlight. "Go ahead. Then I'll simply take the thing and throw it out the window."

Jennifer was dubious. "Oh, sure. Right out the window."

"Just watch me." A button was pressed, and the window on the driver's side slid open.

She blinked in amazement. "You'd do it, wouldn't you? A valuable piece of jewelry like this?"

"What makes you think it's so valuable? For all you know, I found the ring in a box of Crackerjacks."

"I'd love to see the supermarket you bought it in."

There was a long pause. "Seriously, Jennifer. It would make me happy if you'd just accept the ring as a gift . . . from an old family friend."

"A rather extravagant gift, wouldn't you say?"

"Please." Seth drew off his glasses and studied her face with quiet intensity. "I don't get married every day, even if it's only for make-believe. I have every right to give my bride-to-be a wedding gift, don't I?"

"Yes, but—" Jennifer stopped. For what reason was she carrying on this way? At the end of one year, which was approximately how long the marriage would exist on paper, she would simply return the ring to Seth Garrison. Why make such a fuss? The man had already turned down ten million dollars. To protest about anything else now would be splitting hairs. "Of course I'll wear the ring," she conceded graciously.

"That's more like it," came the lofty retort. "Now, about Sunday . . ."

They spent the next half hour discussing logistics for the wedding ceremony and made plans to meet again the next evening. There were still many details that needed to be taken care of during the next several days. Seth assured Jennifer that they would certainly manage, and then he walked her up the steps to the glass doors of the main lobby.

"It's been a long day for you, hasn't it?" he inquired softly.

"I expect you feel the same way."

Seth ignored the remark. Instead, he said, "I'll come over after nine o'clock, if that's not too late. There's a meeting I can't get out of, unfortunately."

"I appreciate you coming by at all," she said, aware of a strange tension in the air. "Thanks for everything, Seth. You have no idea what this all means to me."

Seth's lanky frame hovered just inches away from her. "On the contrary, I can just imagine what it means." He seemed to be searching her eyes for something. "I'm here because I want to help you, Jennifer."

There was something so sincere in his words that she was truly touched. Impulsively she reached up and flung her arms around his neck. "Thank you for coming through for me, Seth. I'll never forget this."

Seth stiffened immediately at the unexpected embrace. He stared down at her, momentarily at a loss for words. "You're quite welcome," he murmured at last.

His lips were very close to her hair, Jennifer thought for no particular reason. It occurred to her how strong his body felt against hers. "Did I say thank you?" she asked in sudden confusion.

"A number of times." Seth's breath was warm against her cheek. Damn, he thought. It was taking every ounce of willpower not to return the embrace. He couldn't believe Jennifer was hugging him like this. All he wanted to do was put his own arms around her slender waist and complete the gesture. If she didn't pull away in another second, he wouldn't be responsible for his actions.

Suddenly self-conscious, Jennifer dropped her arms to her sides. "Excuse me. That was a spontaneous reaction."

"Feel free to be as spontaneous as you like." Seth's voice was curiously unsteady. "To be quite frank, I feel a bit spontaneous myself." He bent down and pressed his lips to her flushed cheek. "Good night, Jennifer."

He turned and walked down the steps, back to his car while Jennifer stared after him in sheer astonishment.

To say that Jennifer spent a sleepless night would be an understatement. After tossing and turning for several hours, she finally gave up all thought of achieving any rest and pulled back the bed covers. She trudged into the kitchen and embarked upon an in-depth inventory of her refrigerator. Except for a wilted stalk of celery, a stale bagel and a jar of mustard, it was empty. The truth was, she hadn't done much shopping in the past few weeks. Her appetite had deserted her, for obvious reasons. Now, for the first time in ages, Jennifer was overwhelmed by a gnawing hunger. Out of a clear blue sky, it seemed, the old numbness had begun to recede. It had absolutely nothing to do with Seth Garrison and the way he had looked into her eyes tonight. Nor was it in any way even remotely connected to the brief but tingling kiss he had bestowed upon her, either. Not at all, Jennifer insisted to herself as she slipped into jeans and a sweatshirt, laced up her high-top sneakers and searched for her car keys. It was perfectly natural to be seized by a sudden urge to go grocery shopping at three o'clock in the morning. As she traveled down to the security garage, Jennifer again wondered *why* Seth had kissed her. He had never impressed her as a particularly demonstrative person, let alone an affectionate one. Now she found herself compelled to start looking at the man in a totally different way, as a disturbingly masculine presence. Jennifer drew in a breath. For the next year, Seth was also going to be a *constant* presence. This was the most unsettling fact of all. When she had first decided to go to Seth with her proposal, it had never occurred to Jennifer that there might be complications. Now she wasn't so sure.

Ten minutes later, Jennifer pulled her car into the parking lot of an all-night supermarket on Beverly Boulevard, located along the eastern border of Beverly Hills. In Los Angeles, a twenty-four-hour food store is a great leveler, a place where people from every stratum of society rub elbows and interact in the most basic of human functions—pursuit of the late-night snack. Where else in our culture would a legendary film star stand patiently in the express checkout line behind a college student in the middle of exam week, a police officer on his break and a middle-aged couple in full evening dress? Jennifer mused.

Tonight was no exception. As Jennifer selected a cart and began her nocturnal cruise through the various aisles, she noticed that the place was populated by its usual cross section of insomniac Californians. And aside from an elderly man who was singing to himself in the middle of the frozen-food section, it was just a typical, subdued crowd. In the produce department alone, Jennifer ran into three people she knew—an acquaintance from her aerobics class, a neighbor from her building and an old schoolmate, the son of a popular television game-show host. They all acknowledged her with glazed eyes and wilted smiles. In the wee hours of the morning, most people were not very gregarious. They were in worlds of their own, distracted by private thoughts and delighted to ignore everyone else as they completed their errands in a semizombielike state. For that reason, even the busiest store had a muted quality that Jennifer found almost therapeutic.

Well, wasn't that why she had really come here? She herself was attempting to divert her mind from a disturbing new problem. Mindlessly she reached toward a shelf and dropped four packages of chocolate-chip cookies into the basket. For the first time in years she felt herself pulled—slowly but surely—by an irresistible new attraction. To a man other than Kevin Stern. Poor Kevin. With every passing day he was becoming more and more like a remnant of a wonderful dream that was dissolving in the morning light. The weight of time was creating a greater and greater distance between Jennifer and the image of the vibrant high-school senior she had loved. Kevin had been the first man to kiss her in a romantic way, yet now Jennifer was finding it hard to remember exactly what those kisses had been like.

She sighed and steered the cart purposefully toward the candy aisle. Her life and dreams for the future seemed a hopeless muddle, a giant question mark. Not too long ago, it had all seemed so logical and clear. She had been the daughter of a rich and powerful man—the sole heir to his great fortune. One day, in the far-off future, she would be expected to take her father's place in his business empire. Ultimately, Jennifer had acknowledged, she would have to find a way to meet this responsibility, but during the interim she would have many years to pursue her own ambitions. She'd had plans to study abroad in Spain, where Washington Irving had been inspired to write his classic collection of tales "The Alhambra." Also, she had been offered a post as a teaching assistant to one of the most highly respected professors at the university. Jennifer considered the position, which would start during the summer semester, a vital step in her quest for a doctorate.

But now all was in doubt. Oliver Ramsey's illness had been sudden but ruthlessly final. The man she had been sure would live forever was gone, and the daughter who had pursued a purely academic existence now realized that there were new responsibilities to assume.

The speed at which all this was happening was the most upsetting aspect of the situation for Jennifer. She stared intently at row upon row of sweets, deciding that chocolate was an essential nutrient at a time as stressful as this. At once she was overcome by a need for the special semisweet candy bars her father had brought home when she'd been little. She missed him even more now, in the middle of the night. She missed the wonderful house where she had grown up. It was still painful to think of Charlotte living there, shattering its serenity with her dissonant manner and her shrill friends. But Oliver Ramsey had stipulated that should his daughter comply with the conditions of the will the home in Bel Air would revert to her in three months' time.

Suddenly Jennifer was seized by a brand-new inner confidence. Yes, she thought firmly, her mouth set in a determined line, Seth was right. She would receive everything that was meant to be hers, and the wonderful house was only part of that legacy.

Jennifer's eyelids were beginning to drag by the time she reached the checkout stand, but her heart was filled with a sense of renewal. All this worrying about conflicting emotions toward Seth Garrison was just the result of stress. The momentary attraction she had felt could be directly attributed to her need for an authoritarian figure. Sure, that was it. She had been so alone, so vulnerable, so distraught. And Seth was there, ready for her to lean on. How easy it was to mistake gratitude for affection.

There were only two customers ahead of her on the line. One was a blue-haired punk rocker holding a sleeping infant tenderly against his leather jacket. The other was an anemic-looking man Jennifer recognized as a famous author—who probably had writer's block, she thought. All in all, perfectly average people. She smiled to herself as she unloaded the groceries onto the counter. Things would be less complicated in the morning. Jennifer was convinced that the next time she saw Seth Garrison she'd have only the most cordial feelings for him. Everything else had been in her head...the product of an overactive imagination.

Chapter Four

Oh, my gosh, Morty, it's *her*! I can't believe it! Get me a piece of paper, a napkin...oh, just rip off a corner of the menu! If I don't get her autograph, I'll simply die!''

In another moment the gushing tourist was hovering over their table, pen in hand. "If you could just sign this for me, Miss Bailey. I'm...that is, my daughter is such a fan of yours."

"Sure." Anita gave a polite smile and began to scribble on the proffered scrap of a luncheon menu.

"If you could just make it out to Delilah..." the woman pleaded.

"Okay. There you go."

"And could you add the name Morty?"

Jennifer watched silently, her lips twitching in amusement. She was used to such things happening every time she and Anita went to a public place. A great deal had been written concerning the trials and tribulations of being a major movie star, Jennifer mused. Very little, on the other hand, had been written about the trials and tribulations of being the *best friend* of a major movie star. It was not an uncommon occurrence to be trampled and ignored by ardent fans desperately trying to catch the attention of their idol.

"Sorry about that," Anita said after the autograph hound had departed triumphantly for her own table. "I guess it was a mistake to come to this place. It's just that I really love the burritos here."

"Forget it." Jennifer shrugged. In most area restaurants that catered especially to a celebrity clientele, great pains were taken to ensure that customers were not disturbed during their meal by well-meaning fans. But famous people didn't care to be restricted just to fashionable dining spots. Like anyone else, they wanted to feel free to grab a hamburger or a tostada anyplace and anytime they pleased. The trouble was that since Anita had skyrocketed to fame in a series of slick science-fiction films there was nowhere she could go without being recognized. Now, as they tried to finish lunch at the tiny Mexican cantina in Santa Monica, even the most polite diners could not resist staring in their direction.

"Anyhow, what's this incredible news you have to tell me?" Anita asked.

Jennifer hesitated. "I don't know where to begin."

"Oh, don't leave me dangling like this!" Anita groaned. "Ever since you called this morning and said you had something major to tell me, I've been going bananas with curiosity! To top it off, you even agreed to meet me for lunch, which for you is strange enough!"

"If you'll be quiet, I'll tell you," Jennifer said, starting to smile.

"So, I'm waiting. What could be so all-fired serious that you couldn't just tell me over the phone?"

"I'm getting married."

"You're what?" Anita's voice shot up three octaves.

"I'm getting married."

"That's what I *thought* you said! I just don't believe it." She paused. "Are you serious?"

"Very." Jennifer started to play with the ice in her soft drink.

"Well, like, when did this happen? Who's the guy?" Anita was completely flustered. "I mean, my own best friend and she doesn't even give me a clue until—"

"It's Seth Garrison. We became engaged yesterday—" Jennifer tossed her shoulders "—and the wedding is Sunday."

"Seth Garrison? Are you for real? I can't believe this. Seth Garrison! The same guy who used to—"

Anita stopped. "What do you *mean* the wedding is Sunday?"

"In the afternoon." Jennifer attempted to sound calm. "If you're free, I was hoping you might come. We'll need a witness."

"If I'm free?" The other woman's voice rose. "*If I'm free?* What kind of a question is that?"

"It's just that it's such short notice, and you always have plans on the weekend—"

"Oh, nice! My best friend in the entire world has an obvious mental breakdown and decides to marry some guy she's seen maybe twice in the past couple of years and you have the nerve to ask me if I'm free?" Anita was adamant. "What possibly could I have planned that's more important than going to your wedding, Jenni? I just can't believe—"

"Believe it."

The young actress eyed her steadily. "Okay, I believe it. *Now* do you want to tell me why you're doing it? You can't tell me it's love at first sight or anything like that. So what the heck is going on?"

"It's very simple, actually."

"Yeah? I'm dying to hear it!" Anita rolled her huge amber eyes expressively. "This ought to be good."

"It's a very long story," Jennifer began.

"Well, you're an English major. Make it a *short* story, and be quick about it. The suspense is killing me!"

Jennifer leaned back against the hard wooden bench. "Remember a couple of weeks ago, how I told you that there were some...complications in the dispersal of my dad's estate?''

Her friend nodded. "Some kind of screwy clause in the will, right?"

"I never told you exactly *how* screwy, did I?" Jennifer sighed and started to tell her companion her real reason for forging a matrimonial alliance with Seth Garrison. When she was finished, Anita just sat there in utter amazement.

"Whew!" she declared at last. "Your father was a wonderful guy, but this is bananas! Do you have any idea what you might be letting yourself in for?"

Jennifer shrugged. "Consider the alternative."

Anita made a face. "Yeah, right. Charlotte gets everything. Boy, that was some choice he gave you!" She paused. "With all due respect to your father, how could he even have seriously considered leaving it all to that witch?"

"I'm sure that wasn't his intention."

"Oh, I suppose not. Still—" Anita hesitated "—you have no idea how diabolical and calculating that woman is. If I know Charlotte, you haven't heard the end of this. Not by a long shot."

Jennifer waved her hand. "There's nothing she can do once I'm officially married to Seth."

"Listen." The other woman grew serious. "I don't mean to upset you, but don't underestimate your stepmother."

"What on earth could she possibly do, Anita?"

"I don't know, but I can tell you one thing for sure. Charlotte hates to lose."

Jennifer gave a yawn. "I've heard this all before, and I'm not going to worry about it."

"Maybe you should. That witch can make a lot of trouble for you, no matter how airtight that will appears to be."

"Let her try."

Anita groaned in exasperation. "Jenni, I'm your best friend since we were six years old. Stop trying to put on your old 'I don't care' routine. It won't cut any ice with me. Now let me tell you. In the past, Charlotte has only dealt with you on the most superficial social level. You've never seen her in action as a businesswoman. She's very competitive, very shrewd and extremely ruthless."

"What else is new?" Jennifer was starting to feel uncomfortable.

"I wish you'd take this seriously. Your stepmother isn't just some dumb bimbo. Actually, she's a very *smart* bimbo. Plus the fact that she also happens to be a very good actress—and I ought to know. She can assume a role, put on the charm and make people do whatever she wants them to do. Believe me, she's an incredible manipulator." There was a painful pause. "She's ruined careers of people who dared to compete with her. Skillfully, so no one realizes that she's responsible, Charlotte can shatter another actress's reputation with a web of innuendo and just the properly placed malicious rumor."

"That sounds positively Gothic."

"Okay, I'm not going to argue with you, Jenni. But Charlotte is bad news that won't go away. If she can find a way to break the will, believe me, you might be in for a rough ride. I don't care how terrific Oliver's lawyers are. Charlotte gets around. She knows where a lot of the bodies are buried, as they say."

Jennifer placed an affectionate arm on her friend's shoulder. "I appreciate your concern, but I'm pretty sure that together Seth and I can handle Charlotte."

Anita looked dubious. "I'm not so sure. She knows some very powerful people."

"So do I."

"Well," Anita conceded, "just as long as you don't take the woman lightly. Gee whiz, how could you have such rotten luck? I had terrific stepmothers. All three of them. I cried each time Dad got divorced."

"Can we change the subject?"

"Oh. I was droning on a bit, wasn't I?" The vivacious redhead cupped her chin in her hands and leaned against the table thoughtfully. "What else can we talk about? I know," she said, her expression brightening. "What would you like for a wedding present? And by the way, it's kind of late notice for a bridal shower."

"That's not necessary," Jennifer murmured. "It's not as if it's a *real* wedding."

"Of course it's a *real* wedding! It's legal, isn't it?"

"Yes, but it isn't ... Well, you know—" the words came out awkwardly "—it's just a business arrangement."

"Really? I thought in a business arrangement money was supposed to change hands. Didn't you just tell me that Seth refuses to take a cent? Doesn't sound too businesslike to me, kid." Anita looked at her curiously.

"He's doing it out of, well, friendship. For my father and for me."

"Hmm, friendship? So now we've progressed from business to friendship. Sounds like a solid basis for marriage. You've sold me. What do you think of silver candlesticks or monogrammed sheets?"

Jennifer retorted, "I don't want any gifts. This marriage is in name only, and it's temporary, do you understand? In the situation, presents would embarrass me."

"A bride should always be treated like a bride," came the wistful reply, "even if the situation is only make-believe. Call me old-fashioned about stuff like that."

"Please, Anita. I mean it."

"Fine. Go ahead, be a killjoy."

Later, as they left the cantina and walked to their cars, Anita hesitated. "There's just one thing that puzzles me. If Seth Garrison isn't doing it for the money, what does he get out of being tied down to you for at least a year?"

"I told you, he's doing it because he's an honest and decent person."

"But what does he *get* out of it?"

Jennifer shook her head and stared off into the distance. Past the towering palm trees of the municipal park, the Pacific Ocean glittered bright blue in the sunshine. "Why does he have to get anything out of it? Can't a person simply have an unselfish motive?"

"No."

"Listen, I trust Seth."

"But how well do you really know him, Jenni?"

"What are you trying to say?"

"I'm not quite sure. It's just that marriage isn't something a man like Seth Garrison would enter into lightly. Think about that before Sunday, all right?"

But what does he get out of it? Those words kept echoing back and forth in Jennifer's mind for the rest of the afternoon. Only a day ago she had considered Seth Garrison obsessed with the pursuit of the almighty dollar. By that evening the man had convinced her he hadn't the slightest intention of accepting the ten-million-dollar payment she had offered him as an inducement. Instead, he had acted insulted by it. It was almost as if marrying Jennifer and helping her win the inheritance was a point of honor to him. Despite the doubts that Anita had conveyed after their lunch together, Jennifer felt she should trust her instincts—the inner sense that told her Seth was an honorable man. Yet she was unable to shake the feeling that there was another piece to this complicated puzzle. Something that lay just beneath the surface and was out of reach.

Resigned to the fact that not everyone's life could be an open book, Jennifer occupied her mind with plenty of errands. She stopped off at the campus to visit Professor Lovitt. A plump, happy cherub of a man, he was considered one of the greatest living authorities on the American authors of the nineteenth century. The professor had recently spent an entire sabbatical writing an opera based on *The House of Seven Gables*. He was one of those brilliant eccentrics who embraced life as a series of wonderful possibilities. Others found his enthusiasm contagious. Delighted to see one of his favorite students, he once again urged Jennifer to accept the position as his teaching assistant. Though sympathetic about her current difficulties, he obviously hoped she would make up her mind as soon as possible.

But Jennifer still did not know what her answer would be. It was all a question of what would now be expected of the heiress to Ramsey Enterprises. The pressure was getting to be a bit much, and the last thing she wanted to do, at least for the moment, was make any more decisions. Therefore Jennifer devoted the remainder of the day to an activity that required scarcely any brainpower at all—shopping. Just a mind-diverting stroll through the various levels of the Beverly Center, a multitiered upscale mall—the most popular of its kind in the entire city.

Not that there was anything she wanted or needed to buy, of course. There was just something so irresistibly cheerful about a place bustling with babies and schoolchildren. The former stared wide-eyed from their trendy strollers, and the latter all seemed to be eating frozen yogurt or ice-cream cones as they raced past other shoppers, all the while giggling and shouting to their friends.

Jennifer was able to successfully forget her problems and enjoy an hour of inner tranquillity. Then she paused in front of a jewelry shop where a number of diamond rings glittered behind the glass. Immediately she was reminded of the impending wedding... of Seth Garrison... of Charlotte. Jennifer looked down at her naked left hand. It had not occurred to her until that very moment that she had neglected to wear the engagement ring. It still lay in its velvet box atop a stack of magazines on her coffee table, where she had left it the night before.

Seth stood in the doorway holding a bottle of wine. "Sorry to be late," he said. He was dressed in—what else?—another perfectly cut dark suit and immaculate shirt.

"No problem." Jennifer ushered him inside, wondering if the man owned anything but suits. She almost felt self-conscious in her pastel sweatshirt and snug, faded jeans. But there was no mistaking Seth's appreciative stare as his silver-blue eyes silently took in her appearance.

He handed her the gift-wrapped bottle, which turned out to be champagne. "I thought we could both use this, especially if your day has been anything like mine."

"Thank you," Jennifer said graciously. She was too tactful to tell him that in truth her day hadn't been half-bad. She was also reluctant to mention that except for last night's dinner at Marcello's it had been a long time since she had drunk anything more alcoholic than diet soda. But perhaps tonight she would make another exception. Those disturbing feelings Jennifer had hoped were just part of her imagination were back again. As soon as she had opened the door of her apartment and seen Seth standing there an odd sensation had hit her stomach. It was almost a flashback to when she had been sixteen years old, opening the front door of the Ramsey mansion to find Kevin Stern ready to take her on their first date. For the first time in nine years, Jennifer was actually experiencing butterflies.

Seth glanced at her curiously. "Is something the matter? If you don't particularly care for champagne, it's no problem. I'll just go around the corner and get something else."

"No, this is just fine," she murmured quickly.

"Are you sure?"

"Positive. In fact, if you'll excuse me for a moment, I'll get the glasses."

"Great!" The man's solemn expression brightened considerably.

Damn, thought Jennifer. It hadn't been her imagination! He *was* attractive. And to make matters worse, there was the chronology. Yesterday afternoon, in his office, Seth Garrison had seemed *somewhat* attractive. During dinner he had been *very* attractive. And now, to Jennifer's chagrin, he had become *extremely* attractive. *Incredibly* attractive. *Heart-stoppingly* attractive—eyeglasses and all. Terrific. Wonderful! Did she really need this kind of aggravation? With all the problems she had now, the last thing she needed to confuse matters was some silly schoolgirl crush. A crush on Seth Garrison, of all people! Her self-imposed social exile had certainly taken its toll, Jennifer mused cynically. She wondered if her make-believe bridegroom-to-be had any idea of how vulnerable she was right now.

After Seth opened the champagne, they sat together on the living-room couch going over some last-minute details. Both of them seemed to go out of their way to use words such as *blood tests*, *wedding announcements* and *simple gold band* as impersonally as possible. But there were other words that were considerably more awkward, due to the intimacy implicit in their meanings.

The first one came up rather unexpectedly when Seth quietly asked, "Would you be interested in a honeymoon?"

If he had thrown a hand grenade in the middle of the living room, Jennifer could not have been more astounded. "Do you feel that's really necessary?" She tried to sound as casual as possible.

"That's what I'm asking you," came the smooth reply.

"For the sake of appearances?"

"Of course. What other reason would there be, Jennifer?" He set down his champagne glass on the coffee table and studied her flushed face intently.

She gave a self-conscious laugh. "I can't imagine where we could go."

His eyes didn't leave her face. "Actually, there's a lovely place I know in Carmel. We could fly up there for a few days."

"With your busy schedule, you'd be willing to take all that time off?" Jennifer forgot to feel awkward for just a moment, and she stared at Seth incredulously.

"Yes. I'd *make* the time, Jennifer." He paused significantly. "If *you* wanted me to."

"Oh." That same odd sensation started up again inside her stomach.

"Do you want me to?" came the gentle inquiry. "After all, every bride deserves a honeymoon."

"But then, I won't be a real bride."

"Yes, you will be on Sunday, when the judge makes you Mrs. Seth Garrison. Legally."

"What about technically?" The words were out of Jennifer's lips before she could prevent them. Perhaps it was her nerves, or perhaps the champagne had gone to her head.

"Technically?" Seth choked. "What are you trying to say?"

"I'm only trying to point out that, to put it delicately, a honeymoon exists for the purpose of consummating a marriage . . . not, in my opinion, for the sake of appearances."

Shakily the man next to her reached for the bottle and refilled both their glasses, splashing some of the golden liquid all over the coffee table. "Are you saying that you want a *real* honeymoon, Jennifer?"

Instantly mortified at the misunderstanding, she flushed an even deeper shade of pink. "No! Absolutely not!" Nervously she reached for her champagne glass, and took several gulps. "That's not what I meant at all!"

"What do you mean, then?" There was a strange note in his voice.

"Just that, well, I don't believe either of us should have to turn our lives completely upside down. That is . . . we needn't drop everything and disappear up the Coast for a few days because we don't want to arouse people's suspicions."

"Won't it be considered—" he hesitated "—odd, if the two of us don't go somewhere after the wedding?"

Jennifer lowered her eyes and stared at the carpet. "Frankly, I don't care what other people think. Anyway, nowadays it isn't unusual for many newlyweds to put off their honeymoons, or even postpone them indefinitely. Besides, from what I understand, your work schedule is so hectic that even the nosiest of the nosy wouldn't question Mr. Seth Garrison going back to the office immediately after the ceremony.''

''Fine,'' came the abrupt answer. ''No honeymoon, then, if that's how you feel about it.''

''But I honestly appreciate the fact that you were prepared to take the time off, Seth. That was rather generous.''

''Forget it.''

''Is there anything else we haven't covered?''

''As a matter of fact, there is something.'' He cleared his throat. ''A subject we haven't discussed up until now.''

''I can't imagine what.''

He set down his wineglass abruptly and looked Jennifer squarely in the eye. ''The subject of living arrangements.''

''What do you mean?'' She was openly confused.

He paused. ''I cannot believe that your attorneys failed to make this matter clear to you, but Oliver's will is quite specific. According to the conditions, we must live together as man and wife.'' There was a long silence. ''Surely you were aware of that, Jennifer?''

''I didn't think that aspect was completely... necessary.''

''Well, it *is* completely necessary, I can assure you.''

Jennifer felt herself losing control of the situation. ''Are you trying to tell me that we're actually going to have to *live* together?''

Seth nodded. ''What did you expect?''

She threw up her hands. "I have my home and you have yours. Just as with the honeymoon, I don't see why we have to keep up that kind of facade. That's going a bit too far."

"I disagree."

"Oh, really?"

"Because this is different. The honeymoon aspect is, as you say, strictly a matter of appearances. But a marriage where the spouses do not cohabit causes a great many questions. Too many, in fact."

"And I suppose you have that on the best legal advice?" Jennifer continued to protest stubbornly.

"The very best," he asserted. "But all that aside, might I also remind you that the fewer questions anyone asks, the better. Particularly Charlotte."

"I'm not worried about Charlotte," she maintained. Who was she kidding? Hadn't Anita's warnings actually reinforced Jennifer's fears about the woman? Of course she was worried, no matter how strongly she tried to deny it.

"Be that as it may—" Seth shrugged "—common sense should at least convince you that to give our marriage even the slightest degree of validity, living in the same home is essential." His voice softened. "Listen, I know this is not quite what you had in mind in your version of a name-only marriage. This is for the sake of appearances, Jennifer. After all, only *we* know what the reality is."

"But it's nobody else's business!"

"In this case, it could be." His mouth was set in a hard line. "I suggest you have another talk with your lawyers, because according to them your father's will does not recognize a marriage of convenience."

"But I thought—"

"That as long as you married someone in a legal ceremony nothing further in the way of formalities need be observed? Well—" his tone was mildly sarcastic "—I hate to burst your bubble, but as Oliver Ramsey's daughter you should have had a more sophisticated grasp of the situation."

"It's not necessary to be insulting."

"Forgive me," Seth said, "but I must be completely honest with you, Jennifer. You're simply not being realistic."

There was no doubting the man's sincerity, Jennifer was forced to admit. And he *did* have a very persuasive point. Perhaps, deep down, she had always known that this concession could not be avoided. She released a long sigh. "So I guess there's no getting out of it. We're going to have to live together."

"Yes." He gazed at her steadily. "For a while, anyway."

"Terrific."

"I can understand this is a major inconvenience," came the frank reply, "but if I'm willing to put up with it, then you should also."

Jennifer felt ashamed of herself for quibbling over this point. Seth was going out on a limb for her sake. Of course he was right...as always. It was just that she had lived alone for so long that it seemed impossible to imagine sharing a space with anyone else—especially a virtual stranger. She could feel her treasured calm and private space shrinking away even now. ''You're right,'' she finally murmured.

Seth managed the slightest hint of a smile. ''It won't be the end of the world, Jennifer.''

She quirked an eyebrow. ''You're absolutely sure you won't mind living with me for a few months?''

''Absolutely.'' His smile grew ironic. ''Believe me.''

''It's just that my apartment is somewhat small for—''

Unexpectedly he reached out and covered her hand with his own. ''You'll be moving into my place, of course.''

''Oh.'' Jennifer suppressed a quiver.

''There's plenty of space for us both to be quite comfortable, I assure you.'' The pressure from his hand was gentle yet warm. ''My guest bedroom is very pleasant.''

''You're sure it isn't an . . . intrusion?''

''Very sure.''

She pulled her hand away and nervously ran her fingers through her long hair. ''When should I move in, then?''

''Anytime you want.'' There was a pause. ''How about tonight?''

''You're joking, of course.''

But Seth's expression told another story. ''You're welcome in my house now, Jennifer,'' he murmured, reaching into the inside pocket of his suit and pulling out a set of keys. "You're always welcome for as long as you wish." He caught her hand again and gently pressed the keys into her palm. "Appearances or not, it's your home for as long as you need it."

Jennifer felt curiously light-headed all of a sudden. "Thank you," she managed finally. "I think that sometime after Sunday is a good idea. I'll need to get everything organized."

"Take all the time you need." His voice was low. "And let me know how I can help. I'm excellent at carrying suitcases," he added.

"I'm sure I'll do fine on my own." Jennifer's smile was faint. He was being so nice. So helpful. Almost endearing! Against her will she was being drawn to the man, more and more with every passing minute. She would have preferred the relationship to be cut-and-dried. Jennifer wasn't quite sure how to handle a *warm* Seth Garrison. It was going to be awkward enough sharing a house with the man. But *liking* him was another complication altogether.

He seemed to be waiting for her to say something else. When she didn't, he shrugged and stood up. Beside the couch, he towered above her. "Well, I mustn't keep you from whatever it is you have to do."

Jennifer was taken off guard. "You aren't keeping me from anything."

For a moment Seth appeared to consider her words. Then he said hastily, "Anyhow, it's getting late."

"I suppose so." She rose from the couch quickly—too quickly—and lost her balance. In fact, she most certainly would have crashed headlong into the coffee table if Seth had not reached out just in time, catching her as she stumbled. Looking back on it, she wasn't quite sure how it all happened. One moment she was falling, and the next moment she was held in Seth's surprisingly strong arms, pressed up against his chest.

Neither of them said anything for a moment. Seth just stood there, holding her tightly against the soft wool of his jacket. More tightly, it seemed, than was necessary to prevent the average fall. "I think you may have had a little too much champagne." Seth tried to sound calm, but his heart was racing a mile a minute. Pressed to her feminine softness, he was coming dangerously close to losing control. This embrace was far more arousing than that of last evening. Part of him wanted to pull away before he made a complete fool of himself, but another part of him was savoring the delightful sensation of holding Jennifer in his arms. And that part of him had absolutely no intention of letting her go. Not yet, anyway. It was a kind of sweet torture.

"I'm not normally a champagne drinker," she was murmuring against his smooth white oxford-cloth shirt. "This is highly unusual for me." In an attempt to steady herself, Jennifer began to draw back.

"Wait," Seth whispered. "Just let me hold you for a minute." One firm hand came to rest along the small of her back, and the other gently cupped her chin.

"What are you doing?" she breathed in a voice that wasn't her own.

"Remember what you said last night about being spontaneous? Well—" one of his fingers traced the outline of her lips "—I'm being spontaneous, Jennifer." At once he lowered his mouth to hers in a hard, brief kiss that left her senses tingling, an electrifying shock of a kiss that was over almost before it had begun. Seth pulled back almost immediately, a stunned expression on his gaunt face. "Then again, perhaps being spontaneous isn't always such a good idea."

Jennifer struggled to regain what was left of her composure. "Perhaps you're right." Unconsciously she put a hand to her flushed cheek.

"Good night," he said in a hoarse voice. "I'll call you tomorrow. Take care of yourself, Jennifer."

Chapter Five

They were married on Sunday. Judge Helmer, a balding gentleman in his early fifties, performed the brief ceremony in the living room of Seth's Benedict Canyon home. There were only two witnesses. One was Anita, and the other was a relative of Seth's who had flown in from out of town. Both of them observed the proceedings in respectful silence, lending their quiet support to the bride and groom.

Jennifer saw Seth only one more time before the wedding. At that meeting he seemed strangely remote and impersonal, rather like the serious young Mr. Garrison she remembered from her childhood. It was obvious to Jennifer that he regretted kissing her the other evening. Since she also had mixed feelings about the incident, it was just as well to forget that the brief kiss had ever happened. Upon reflection, Jennifer was quite convinced that the startling chemistry of the moment was the product of champagne and nervous anxiety—a potent combination, to be sure. In any case, neither of them referred to it again, and Seth seemed to go out of his way to avoid even the most casual physical contact. There were no more reassuring touches on her shoulder, or even the slightest handshake.

"Then by the authority vested in me by the state of California, I pronounce you husband and wife." The judge gave both of them a warm smile and added, "You may now kiss the bride." He waited expectantly.

There was a prolonged pause. Then, almost reluctantly, the newlywed couple exchanged a most perfunctory kiss and quickly drew apart, both ill at ease.

"Congratulations," Anita murmured, embracing each of them hastily. Seth's cousin Daniel, a quiet-spoken lawyer from New York, repeated Anita's gesture. Like her, he seemed to instinctively understand the awkwardness of the situation. "My best wishes to you both." The man grasped Jennifer's cold fingers and held them reassuringly for a moment. "You couldn't have found a better man than Seth," he said. Then he added, "Under any circumstances."

With champagne, everyone toasted the health of the bride and groom. Jennifer barely touched her lips to the goblet, unable to do anything but pretend to take a swallow. While the others' conversation faded into the background, a dull throbbing grew louder and louder in her head. Blindly Jennifer stared out the floor-to-ceiling window, into the garden.

Seth's hillside home was a modern structure of redwood and glass with a dramatic view of the city below. Built in the late sixties by a renowned architect, the house had a design based on the bow of a ship. One portion was curved to enclose a small swimming pool. It was an ingenious use of a limited amount of space to create an environment of privacy. At another time and in different circumstances, Jennifer would have been able to appreciate the serene beauty of this stunning contemporary showplace, but now nothing was farther from her mind.

I am actually married. The thought continued to pound inside her brain. *I am a married woman.* And even though the marriage was just a formality, it signified to Jennifer the end of an era in her life. A final farewell to the freedom from responsibility. And something else, too. She looked down at the third finger of her left hand. Next to the sparkling diamond engagement ring was a plain gold band. Over the years, whenever Jennifer had imagined her wedding day, it was always with the smiling image of her first and only love standing beside her. In all those fantasies it had been Kevin, his eyes laughing back at her—the one wonderful dream that had somehow managed to stay alive in Jennifer's heart. But now the wistful dreams of girlhood were truly ended. It was time to put the fantasy of Kevin away forever. In many ways, Jennifer had stopped mourning him long ago, yet in other ways the pain had never left.

An incredible new sensation of sadness overwhelmed her as she gazed past the eucalyptus trees toward the bright sun. Jennifer's eyes began to water. Just for a moment the bittersweet memory of Kevin flared to life again. How well she could now understand the tears in the eyes of an old man when he suddenly confronted a reminder of a long-dead loved one. But just as quickly as the sadness had come, it was gone. Her heart now accepted what her mind already knew. This afternoon, after seven years, Jennifer had finally said goodbye to Kevin Stern.

"Are you all right?" a quiet voice asked.

Surprised, she turned around to see Seth. How long had he been standing there? Jennifer wondered. "I'm fine."

"Really?" Seth took a white linen handkerchief out of his pocket and dabbed gently at several stray tears just beginning their journey down her cheek.

"The sun is so bright," Jennifer explained lamely, "it made my eyes water."

Seth arched an eyebrow but made no comment. He took back the monogrammed square, refolded it and slipped it inside the front pocket of his immaculate suit. With an ironic sigh, he said, "I thought we had an understanding to do our best to be honest with each other."

She smiled brightly. "Like I said, I'm fine now."

"Jennifer..." He took her hand in his. "Listen to me. Don't you think I know what you're probably feeling right now? Of course—" he paused significantly "—I can imagine who and what you were thinking about, and the sadness you feel. Believe me—" his silver-blue gaze was openly compassionate "—I understand. I know this wasn't a choice you made happily."

Jennifer sighed. "I'm sorry, I—" But there were no words. There was nothing else to say. The emotion of the moment was too strong.

Seth compressed his lips in a tight line. "Come here," he rasped suddenly, pulling her into a tender embrace.

"I'm sorry," she repeated against his rough wool sleeve, unable to stop trembling.

"I promise," he whispered into her hair, "I'm going to help you get through this thing, honey." He added, "We'll both get through it all right."

Jennifer continued to tremble, but for a different reason. In the midst of her vague sadness, Seth's endearment pierced the pain surrounding her heart. It was the first and only endearment she had ever heard him use. And in all the times of her life when she'd heard anyone else use the same word, it had never seemed as heartfelt or genuine as it did coming from this usually brusque man. *Honey.* "I'm not worried," she breathed against the warmth of his chest. "It's just that everything happened so fast. I feel so...odd."

"Maybe we both do," he confessed softly, brushing a stray wisp of blond hair away from her forehead. "It's kind of an odd situation, isn't it?"

"Well, at least we got through the wedding."

"Yes. So far, so good," he agreed, and drew back, resting both hands on her shoulders.

Jennifer felt the heat of his fingers through the thin blue silk of her dress. Catching a brief glimpse of the shiny gold band on one of those tanned, firm fingers, she recalled something that had surprised her at the time. In an unexpected gesture, Seth had chosen to wear a wedding ring, as well. "I appreciate what you're trying to do," she told him now, "but you don't have to wear a ring if you don't want to."

"I want to."

"Really, it's not necessary."

"No." He studied her face with an impenetrable silver stare. "I insist. Besides, if you have to wear a wedding band, so should I."

Jennifer considered his remark thoughtfully. "I suppose you realize that wearing it might cramp your...style."

"Yours, too," he tossed back in a dry voice. "But then, married people—at least *newly* married ones—shouldn't be worried about such things, should they?"

"Yes, but—"

"In fact," Seth declared forcefully, "it might be a sensible idea to refrain from any, shall we say, 'extra-curricular socializing' for the time being."

"I wasn't talking about myself. That is, I had no intention of seeing other men while we—" Jennifer stopped her protest when she saw the smile spreading across Seth's gaunt face.

"Well, then, give me a little credit, too," he countered.

"I don't really know you very well."

"You will. Come to think of it, one day you might even understand me." His fingers traveled down her blue silk sleeves. "By the way, you look very lovely in that dress, Jennifer."

"Thank you." She smiled up at him sincerely. "It was nice of you to bring flowers," she said, referring to the elegant spray of white baby roses pinned to the back of her chignon.

"My pleasure," he murmured.

"Are the two of you going to loiter over there forever," Anita called out teasingly, "or are we going to honor our luncheon reservations?"

Judge Harold Helmer gave Anita one last admiring stare before regretfully leaving to perform another wedding. That left the newlyweds, accompanied by Anita Bailey and Daniel Garrison, to celebrate over lunch. They dined at one of Los Angeles's most exclusive restaurants, tucked discreetly in the hills above Malibu. Although rustic, the place had an indefinable aura of elegance and charm. The table waiting for them was the best in the establishment, by the broad bay window, with a panoramic view of the Pacific.

The meal itself was a lighthearted, pleasant affair, due to the company. The two wedding guests were the dearest friends of the bride and groom, and they kept the conversation bright and lively. It was a measure of Anita and Daniel's sensitivity to the situation that neither one made romantic or risqué innuendos concerning the newly married couple. It was also true that Anita was still Anita, and despite the fact that he was successful and confident in his own right, Daniel Garrison was obviously overwhelmed by the fact that he was actually sitting and having lunch with a beautiful movie star.

Occasionally Jennifer could feel Seth's eyes watching her, but she no longer felt self-conscious about it. It was a pleasant sensation knowing that he found her attractive. And what had started as an awkward, worrisome afternoon was evolving into a relaxing, happy evening. That is, until she caught sight of a familiar slender figure being seated by the maître d' at a nearby table.

Jennifer's heart sank. *Charlotte*. Damn, she thought. What a way to ruin a person's day. Desperately she glanced at Seth, who was also aware of the woman's presence.

"It's all right," he murmured reassuringly, taking her hand. "Don't worry about her."

"How can I *not* worry about her? She's staring right at us!"

"In that case, I suppose we ought to give her something worth staring at," Seth reasoned. Without another word, he leaned over and draped his arm over her shoulder.

The stunning red-haired actress gaped at them from her own table, then suddenly rose from her chair and strode across the room. Charlotte DeLeon Ramsey was an older version of Anita Bailey, only glossier and less endearing. Even at thirty-seven, Charlotte's perfect, supple body was the envy of Hollywood. On sheer looks alone, no one in the business could match her. But character? Well, that was another story altogether.

"Look who's here." She stood before them, speaking in a voice that positively dripped sweet venom. "My adorable friends. Why, if it isn't the princess herself." She glared at Jennifer. "And I do believe she's found herself a frog prince!" Charlotte's green eyes flashed at Seth.

"Hey, Charlotte!" Anita made a heroic attempt to divert the intruder's attention. "I didn't recognize you without your broomstick."

"Oh, they're all here—frogs *and* toads. It must be an epidemic!" Charlotte turned her glance back to Jennifer. "So it's true," she hissed, noting the single white rose on Seth's lapel and both wedding rings. "You're married."

The anger began to boil inside Jennifer, but before she could make a caustic retort, Seth's arm tightened around her reassuringly.

"Either congratulate us or leave," he uttered in a tone so cold that even his cousin stared at him in amazement. "You aren't welcome here, Charlotte."

The perfectly painted iridescent pink lips smiled. "Let's cut the amenities, shall we? I know what the two of you are trying to pull, and you're not going to get away with it!"

"Why don't you mind your own business?" Anita said with a glare.

Charlotte ignored the outburst and continued to vent her hostility on Seth and Jennifer. "Do you two think I'm dumb enough to swallow this phony marriage routine?"

"Whatever are you talking about?" Seth inquired with icy calm. "Phony marriage?" He turned to Jennifer. "Did you hear that, sweetheart? Your wonderful stepmother thinks we aren't really married."

"But *darling*," Jennifer said, playing along, "wherever would she get such an absurd idea?"

Charlotte rolled her eyes. "You really believe I'm some kind of moron?"

"Absolutely." Anita blew a wall of cigarette smoke at her. "Why should we be different from the rest of the world?" She winked at Daniel Garrison, whose lips twitched involuntarily.

"Stay out of this," warned Charlotte through clenched teeth. "I'm in no mood for second-rate theatrics from a third-rate starlet."

"Starlet?" Anita practically exploded. "When was the last time you read *Variety*? I understand they can't *give* away tickets to your movies—"

Jennifer gave a discreet cough. "I wish you'd leave, Charlotte. You're ruining an otherwise happy occasion." She looked at Seth. "Isn't that right, darling?"

"Oh, *please*!" Charlotte's eyes were narrow green slits. "This is all about as convincing as a school play. You think I don't know an acting job when I see one?"

"Who's acting?" Seth lowered his voice and stared into his bride's hazel eyes. "Have you any idea how crazy I am about you, Mrs. Garrison?"

"Give me a break," Charlotte snarled. "If you two cold fish feel anything for each other, I'll laugh myself silly." She paused. "By the way, once I prove that this little charade of yours is a fake, the last laugh is going to be mine."

"Cold fish?" Jennifer repeated to her new husband with a conspiratorial wink. "Did you hear what she said?"

"Cold fish, indeed," Seth murmured. And right there, in the restaurant, he pulled her directly onto his lap.

Charlotte actually raised an eyebrow as Jennifer responded by placing her arms possessively around Seth's neck. "Charade, indeed," the new Mrs. Garrison said, somewhat shakily. "Whatever is the matter with that woman?"

"I don't know—" Seth reached out and cupped her chin "—and I don't care." Something strange glittered in his silver-blue eyes as he pulled off his glasses and tossed them casually onto the table. "I only want to kiss you, sweetheart."

Seth brought his mouth down on hers at once. The contact was as electric as it had been that night in Jennifer's apartment, but much more intense. This was no brief brush of the lips. He kissed her long and hard, and Jennifer couldn't help but respond. With her eyes closed, she yielded to the sweet surprise of his demanding mouth, winding her arms even more tightly around Seth's neck. Somewhere along the line, it all ceased to be playacting. She sighed and parted her lips against the tentative exploration of his tongue, savoring the marvelously male taste of him. He smelled of soap and spicy after-shave, that traditional masculine combination that held a startling potency on Seth. Of her own volition, Jennifer reached up to caress the tense cord at the back of his neck, traveling farther to run curious fingers through his thick brown hair.

Seth drew a shocked breath and looked down at her in utter astonishment. "Jennifer!"

At once her eyelids fluttered open and met his stunned expression head-on. "What's the matter?" she whispered softly. "Do you think we might have overdone it?"

"That's one way to put it," he declared faintly, observing her flushed cheeks and bright eyes. "Where did you learn how to kiss, anyhow?"

In a low voice that was audible only to him, Jennifer replied, "You don't think it needs work? Actually, I'm a bit rusty."

"Trust me," came the hoarse reply, "you did just fine."

"I guess it's kind of like falling off a bicycle..." she murmured along the hard line of his jaw.

"Something like that," Seth agreed shakily.

"How touching," Charlotte interrupted in a strident tone. "What an Oscar-winning performance!" Despite the woman's bluster, she was quite clearly confused by the passionate embrace she had just witnessed. "And it proves nothing!"

They were back in the real world again, the spell of their long, intoxicating kiss finally broken. Abruptly Jennifer, bewildered, pulled her lips away from the rough warmth of Seth's cheek, her senses still reeling. He released her with considerable reluctance, his arms dropping to his sides.

"Well, well," Charlotte said, continuing to bait them, "have the lovebirds finished their little display already?"

Seth reached for his eyeglasses and perched them on his chiseled nose again. "Oh, are you still here, Charlotte?"

Barely suppressed fury seethed in Charlotte De-Leon Ramsey's beautiful face. "You haven't heard the end of this," she choked out, "not by a long shot!" Without another word, she stalked back to her own table, where a handsome young man, at least fifteen years her junior, sat idly munching on tortilla chips.

No one said anything for a long, uncomfortable moment. Finally Daniel Garrison remarked, "I'll never be able to watch an old film of hers on television again."

"Yeah," Anita said, nodding sympathetically. "It does kind of shatter the illusion, doesn't it?"

Neither Jennifer nor Seth made a comment aloud, but both were wondering silently to themselves how Oliver Ramsey could ever have married such a distasteful person. What had he possibly seen in her?

It was Daniel Garrison who tactfully found a way to bring the luncheon to a close by announcing that it was growing late and he had a plane to catch. The man knew full well what a tiring and stressful day it had been for the bride and groom. Anita immediately caught on and insisted on driving Seth's cousin to the airport personally.

"It's a mess on the freeway this time every Sunday," she explained blithely. "I know all the back roads, so you won't miss your flight."

"That's . . . very kind of you," Daniel murmured in surprise, and gratefully accepted the offer.

Later on, when the two of them were alone, Jennifer felt the old awkwardness returning again. Seth had brought her back to her apartment and walked with Jennifer only as far as the front door.

"Well, I suppose I'll be seeing you tomorrow," he said quietly. "Unless there's anything you'd like me to help you with now." He paused. "What I mean is, can I take any boxes or suitcases back with me tonight?"

"No, thanks." Jennifer had the feeling he was waiting for her to do or say something, but she was almost afraid to guess what that might be. Instead, she remarked lightly, "I like your cousin Daniel. It was very nice of him to treat us all to lunch."

"I'd say he had a rather good time," Seth observed with a twist of his lips. "It isn't often that Dan gets a ride to the airport from a gorgeous movie star."

Something inexplicable stabbed at Jennifer. "Yes, Anita is very beautiful, isn't she?"

"Very," Seth agreed in a low voice, "but not as beautiful as you are, Jennifer." And with that he turned and walked down the steps to his car. In another moment his Mercedes screeched out of its parking space and tore quickly down the street, disappearing into the dusk.

Thus went Jennifer Garrison's wedding day.

Chapter Six

Jennifer accomplished her move to Seth Garrison's canyon home within three days. She astonished even herself with her efficiency.

First she placed all her furniture and posters and most of her other household items in storage. With the exception of her clothes, some books and a few articles Jennifer considered precious, she could get by without most of her possessions for the next few months. The plan, as far as she was concerned, would be to move back into the Ramsey mansion when Charlotte was legally obligated to vacate the residence. Jennifer had not yet discussed this plan with Seth, but she was sure he would agree. On the third day after the wedding, Jennifer packed her suitcases, along with whatever boxes could fit into the back seat

and trunk of her car, and drove over to Seth's house.
The move was completed as simply as that, while he
was at work. Seth seemed somewhat surprised that
Jennifer preferred not to ask for his assistance. For
reasons best known to himself, he decided against
pushing the issue.

When he arrived home from the office that evening, he found his new bride comfortably ensconced
in the large, pleasant guest room located at the back
of the house. The room's pastel carpet was thick and
soft. The walk-in closet was more than adequate for
her wardrobe, and the built-in shelves suited her collection of books admirably. What made the accom-
modations especially nice was the sliding glass door
leading out to the swimming pool. Maybe, Jennifer
thought hopefully, stretching out on the queen-size
bed, living in this place for the next several months
wouldn't be that bad after all.

"Jennifer."

She looked up from the pillows to see Seth standing
in the open doorway, the jacket to his suit slung across
his shoulder. This was about as casual as she had ever
seen him look. "Oh, hello." Jennifer smiled and ges-
tured toward the boxes strewn across the bedroom
floor. "As you can see, I'm not quite settled in yet."

"May I come in?"

"What kind of a question is that? It's your house."

"But it's *your* room."

"Oh, please! Why should you even have to ask?"
She rolled her eyes in a perfect imitation of Anita

Bailey. "Come in, and don't ask silly questions." At ease for the first time in weeks, Jennifer crossed her denim-clad legs casually on top of the bedspread.

Seth shrugged and took a few steps inside. "I'm just trying to respect your...space, as they say these days."

"If you really want to make me feel at home, Seth, you won't stand on ceremony."

"All right." He hesitated. "But I just want to ensure your privacy, Jennifer." He was reluctant to admit aloud what a delightful sensation it was to come home from work and find Jennifer there. Call him a male chauvinist, call him sexist—oh, just call him an old-fashioned romantic—but in his fantasies about Jennifer, this was what Seth had always imagined. They were married, and here she was, waiting for him to return from work. He let his daydreams stray even more and imagined the two of them having dinner in the glass-walled dining alcove, watching the sun set slowly in the west. *Damn, here I am being poetic again,* he chastised himself. If he wasn't careful, he would start mistaking his fantasies for reality. Bad enough, he thought, to see her relaxing in one of his own beds. Worse to tantalize himself with the searing memory of the passionate kiss they had exchanged in the restaurant Sunday night. There was safety in the fact that Jennifer believed he was playacting. He would never tell her how real that kiss had been for him, or that her unexpectedly enthusiastic response had almost pushed him over the edge. Part of him wanted desperately to believe that it hadn't all been

playacting on Jennifer's part, but common sense told
Seth otherwise. She was beautiful, she was young, she
was bubbling with life. She could have any man she
wanted, so why on earth would she want *him*? Suddenly the confident businessman was an insecure
teenager again, a gangly, sallow-skinned high-school
senior. So what if he was the smartest kid in the class,
the one who delivered the valedictory address? He had
always been considered different. A *nerd*.

"Privacy?" Jennifer was saying. "That's not a very
comfortable way for two people to get along." She
tossed back her long blond hair and looked pensive.
"If we want to keep this arrangement easy and pleasant, let's pretend we're back in college and this is a
dorm." She smiled sincerely. "And you and I are
roommates."

"Roommates?" Seth sounded skeptical. Jennifer
was not like any roommate he had ever had! That was
for sure.

"If you don't mind, I'd like to keep this as informal as possible, Seth. I mean, sure, we'll do our best
to stay out of each other's way when necessary, but if
we're continually asking permission to come into
rooms when the door is already wide open, well—"
Jennifer was sincerely concerned "—that's going to
make life around here very awkward."

"I don't want to make anything uncomfortable for
you." Seth took several strides toward her and sat
down on the edge of the wide bed. "That's the last
thing I want, believe me." Lord, she was adorable

right now, he was thinking. Without makeup she looked like a teenager. A very shapely, alluring teen-ager, of course. What would Jennifer say if he reached out right now and let his fingers sift through that silky blond hair? He tortured himself further. What would she say if he leaned over and kissed that sweet mouth of hers again? Only this time it wouldn't be in the safety of a crowded restaurant. They were alone here. Alone, Seth thought, continuing his inner torment, in a secluded house. In a bedroom. On a bed. This was insanity! How on earth was he going to keep control during the next few days, let alone the next few months? He cleared his throat. "Have you eaten dinner yet?"

"Actually, I forgot to eat at all today. You know how it is when things get hectic."

"Does my new roommate want to join me for supper? I'm not the worst cook in the world."

Jennifer looked at him in surprise. "You can cook?"

"I'm not Cordon Bleu, but on the other hand I'm not half-bad, either."

"Funny, I never pictured you wearing a chef's apron. I always imagined that you ate most of your meals out."

"There's a lot you don't know about me, Jenni-fer." Seth rolled up the fine cotton sleeves of his white shirt. "I promise you, I can manage in the kitchen." He paused, then continued, "What kind of salad dressing would you prefer on the endive and spinach?''

"Oh, this sounds serious.''

He smiled back at her. "How does veal scaloppine sound, then? Too serious?''

"Not at all. It happens to be a favorite of mine.'' Jennifer quirked an eyebrow. In all the years she had known Seth, he had never seemed so absolutely, well...lighthearted. And something else, too. She had never before seen him without a jacket on. He seemed broader in the shoulders than she had imagined he would be. There was a hard, muscular strength to his bare forearms, and that was unexpected, as well. Jennifer had the absurd impulse to reach over and see for herself just how hard those arm muscles actually were.

For the slightest instant, Seth thought she was looking at him in a way that could almost be construed as flattering, but surely such an idea was ridiculous. Although... He paused to look into those enigmatic hazel eyes.

Hastily Jennifer averted her gaze, staring at the bedspread. "Yes, scaloppine would be lovely.''

"Great, I'll go defrost it, then.'' No, he thought in disappointment. It was all in his mind. Oh well, he sighed inwardly. Why couldn't he have been born handsome like one of the out-of-work actors who populated L.A. like sand on the seashore? Or at least be as good-looking as his cousin Daniel. During their childhood, the girls had always flocked to Daniel, agreeing to a double date only due to the persuasiveness and charm of his cousin. Some things just happened for some people without effort, and that was the story of the world.

"Is there anything I can do to help in the kitchen?" Jennifer was asking now.

"No. Besides, you must be exhausted. Why not just relax for a while? I'll call you when dinner's ready."

"Really, Seth. I'd like to do *something*."

There was a pause. "Well, you could help me drink a bottle of wine while I prepare the vegetables."

"Oh." She wasn't going to make *that* mistake again.

"Is something wrong?"

"Well, it's just that I don't believe anything alcoholic is a very wise idea right now." Who knows what she might say or do after a few glasses of wine this time?

"You'd really like this particular chardonnay. I get it from a friend who owns a small vineyard up north."

"I'd rather not, Seth."

"Sure, no problem." He tried not to sound disappointed. Foolishly he had begun to envision wine and candlelight. Right now Seth wished he had joined one of those gyms near the beach in Santa Monica and pumped iron. So what if he jogged a few miles every morning? Who cared that he'd even run in marathons? What he wouldn't give this moment for rippling biceps. Muscles the size of Omaha, Nebraska. That was what women these days thought were sexy. Oh, who was he kidding? He didn't care about *women*, he only cared about *this* woman. Damn, he groaned to himself again. She was so lovely and sweet. Why did he have to be so commonplace? So boringly nondescript? And, on top of everything else, near-sighted?

"I don't mean to be such a prig about the wine," Jennifer explained, "it's just that I'm trying to cut back."

"I understand completely. Don't worry about it." Why had he never bothered to get contact lenses? Seth wondered.

"You really don't mind?"

"Jennifer, the last thing I'd ever want to do is make you feel uncomfortable in any way. In fact, I want you to let me know if I ever do anything like that at all."

She smiled shyly. "I'm sure that won't be a problem. I think I'll be very comfortable here."

"I was hoping you'd like it."

"You have a beautiful home, Seth. In some ways, it reminds me of my... old home."

He looked skeptical. "How can you say that? This place is nice, but there's absolutely no comparison to—"

"I mean, it's so peaceful and serene."

"I'm glad you feel that way."

Jennifer hesitated, then said in a low voice, "I want to thank you again for helping me."

"My pleasure." Seth stood up. "I'm just glad you're here." Without another word, he walked out of the room, leaving Jennifer staring after him in surprise and puzzlement.

* * *

The last thing Seth wanted to discuss over a sunset dinner with his new bride was business. He poured himself another glass of wine. What he really wanted to talk about was her beautiful hazel eyes, but that was a rather dangerous subject. He also wanted to mention his crazy desire to play hooky from the office tomorrow and take Jennifer to Disneyland, to behave like the mischievous teenager he'd never had a chance to be. But more than anything he wanted to disclose a newfound urge to go dancing, someplace where the music was always slow. It would be the perfect excuse to hold her close to him. That settled it, Seth decided abruptly. It would be much wiser and considerably safer to stick to the dull subject of business. "And what have you decided about those shares of Northern Technologies?" he blurted out suddenly.

Jennifer set down her soft drink and sighed. "To be perfectly frank, I haven't even thought about it. What do *you* think I should do?"

"I think you should sell out while you can. The stock is overvalued as it is."

"I had no idea." Of course she hadn't. What on earth did she know about her father's business holdings, anyhow? She had never even *heard* of Northern Technologies. What she knew about was Washington Irving and Nathaniel Hawthorne. And nineteenth-century Spain. But look at Seth, she thought, studying the man across the table. He seemed so interested, so concerned about the state of the stock market. It was almost embarrassing to admit her own ignorance.

"On the other hand, I'm not trying to suggest doing something rash, but in this situation, with the economy so volatile . . ."

My goodness, Jennifer thought as Seth rambled on so earnestly about hostile takeover bids in the electronics industry, had he always been this cute? Why hadn't she ever noticed him when he was younger? Did some men just become attractive as they got more mature? Why had it taken her so long to appreciate the rugged masculinity of his gaunt, tanned face? And in addition to that, he was a wonderful cook. Dinner was delicious.

"Furthermore, with Oliver no longer at the helm, I can foresee a few defections on the board. Right now, though, the main problem would seem to be the airline stock. At current market value, there's a tendency to—" Seth stopped. "I am rattling on, aren't I? I'm terribly afraid I must be boring you to death."

"Not at all," came the quick reply.

His mouth twisted in a vague smile, and he put down his wineglass. "Now you're being polite. Business can be a dull topic."

"Listen, Seth," she began earnestly, "I admit I never gave it much thought until Dad—that is, until a few weeks ago. What happens to Ramsey Enterprises is important to me, but I really don't know anything. Dad never discussed his work with me. I wouldn't know what to do first."

Seth leaned back in the chrome-and-leather dining-room chair and glanced into the distance. The sun was just disappearing behind the hills. "Oliver was a stubborn man. There were times he actually believed he would live forever. Delegating responsibility was not one of his stronger points."

"I can think of only one person Dad *ever* delegated responsibility to... only one man he trusted to run things for him." Jennifer paused significantly. "We both know who that was, don't we?"

"I suppose..."

"It was you, Seth. I can't imagine anyone who knows more about the day-to-day operations of the company."

"It's been two years," he said, and shrugged. "Things change."

"Not that much." She stood up and walked toward the terrace. How could she begin to ask him, Jennifer wondered, thrusting her hands into the back pockets of her blue jeans. He was busy enough with his own corporation, and it would be such an imposition. But who else could she ask? "I was wondering..."

"Yes?"

"Do you suppose you might...advise me about the business?"

"It would be my pleasure." Seth couldn't understand why Jennifer was suddenly so ill at ease. After all, it was a perfectly reasonable request.

"Look, I'll be honest with you," Jennifer said, striding back to the table and running her fingers nervously through her silky hair. "I'm supposed to step into the chairmanship by the time the board meets again, Seth." She looked at him hopelessly. "I'm in no way prepared for it. I haven't the vaguest idea what's going on—"

"I already said I'd help you," Seth reassured her quietly.

"That's not all. You see, I—" Why couldn't she just come out with what had been on her mind lately? That rebellious little kernel of an idea that seemed to make more and more sense with each passing minute?

"There's more to it, isn't there?"

Jennifer hesitated. Why beat around the bush any longer? Was her brainstorm really so crazy? The worst Seth could do was say no. "All right, the point is, I've gone over and over this, and it keeps coming out the same. I have absolutely no business sense."

"You can learn."

"Certain things can't be learned—not ever. They're instinctive."

"You underestimate yourself, Jennifer."

"On the contrary, the fact is that I don't have the temperament to run Ramsey Enterprises. I never will—" she sighed "—and to be perfectly truthful, I don't think I really want to. As a responsibility, yes, I'd face up to it if necessary. But I have dreams and goals that I don't want to give up yet." She *wanted* that post at the university. She *wanted* her doctorate. How could she allow those things to slip away without a fight? "I'm not the right person to be chairman of the board of Ramsey Enterprises." Jennifer hesitated. "But I know the person who is."

"And who would that be?"

"I'm looking at him."

Seth stared at her in amazement. "What are you trying to say?"

"Do I have to spell it out, Seth? I'm asking if you would take over in the number one spot. There's no one better suited to run the company, and you know it."

"Are you serious?"

"Of course I am." She caught the glimmer of astonishment in his silver-blue eyes. "You already know how much I respect and trust you. My Dad would have been very pleased to have you as his successor."

A muscle in his jaw tensed. "Have you any idea what you're asking?"

"I realize this is pretty presumptuous of me," Jennifer confessed. "After all, you have a highly successful business of your own already, but—"

"That's not what I mean." He exhaled heavily. "Do you have any conception of what it is you're really doing? You can't just give up your chairmanship to me, honey. It isn't right."

"Why not?"

Seth seemed flustered. "Because, well, it simply *isn't*!"

"That's an articulate answer."

"Seriously, Jennifer. Don't you realize the power you would be handing over to me?"

"Yes."

"Aside from the day-to-day decisions, we're talking about major policy changes. These are things you should have a voice in, things you should be deciding."

"On the contrary." She walked over to his chair and placed a slender hand on his shoulder. "These are things *you* should be deciding. No one understands the company like you do, Seth, and that's the truth."

Seth suppressed a shudder, caused not by the staggering nature of the job offer but by the delicious touch of her fingers through the thin cotton shirt. He knew Jennifer was completely unaware of the wild effect her simple gesture was having on his already elevated pulse rate. He cleared his throat. "That may well be, but this is still a rather hasty decision for you to make. You need time—"

"I don't need any more time. My mind is made up."

"But the chairmanship of Ramsey Enterprises!"

"Let me make this quite clear, Seth Garrison. I want you to take the position." She paused. "The only question that remains is whether or not you'll accept it."

"Jennifer," he pleaded, "you're rushing into this."

"Do you want the job or not?" Her tone was deadly serious.

"I'd have to be a fool not to want it," came the honest reply.

"Then you'll take it?"

"I don't know." Of course he wanted it, Seth thought, groaning inwardly. A man who would turn down such an offer ought to have his head examined! "I'll have to think about it."

"When you're finished thinking about it," Jennifer said, stepping away, "I hope your answer will be yes."

"We'll see," he insisted stubbornly. "We'll just have to see."

It was best that she hadn't pushed, Jennifer decided later. After the dishes were cleared away, she tactfully excused herself to take a shower. It was delightful to relax in the unusual hexagonal stall and feel the water spray down on her weary body. As she rinsed the soapy lather from her skin, Jennifer considered Seth's reaction to the offer of the chairmanship. He had seemed truly surprised, yet not wholly displeased by the offer. She wondered why she hadn't thought of the idea sooner. Putting Seth in charge of Ramsey Enterprises was the perfect solution to her problems. He just *had* to accept.

Jennifer turned off the water and squeezed the excess moisture from her dripping hair. She twisted the latch on the thick fiberglass door. Nothing happened. She tried the catch again, and still it wouldn't budge. "Wonderful!" she muttered, and pushed with all her might against the fiberglass. No luck. This was getting very irritating. "Cut it out this minute," Jennifer warned the door, shoving sideways against it again and again, her frustration increasing with every passing second. "You're just a nasty, rotten inanimate object!" she cried out angrily. "Oh, great. Terrific!" Jennifer slammed her fists into the resilient fiberglass several more times, but to no avail. It was beginning to look as if she were going to be trapped there all night when suddenly she heard a loud banging on the bathroom door.

"Are you all right in there?" Seth called out.

"No, I'm stuck," she shouted back. "Something's wrong with the shower door."

"Do you mind if I come in and help open it for you?"

Did he even have to ask? "Yes, please!" But then Jennifer remembered she was naked. She turned crimson with embarrassment. Well, how else was she supposed to get out of there? The outer door opened, and the blurred figure of Seth grew larger and larger as he advanced toward the semiopaque swirled fiberglass.

"Is it the latch again?"

"You mean it's happened before?"

"Once or twice," Seth declared. "It has something to do with the humidity, I think. All right, I'm going to pull, and I want you to push at the same time. Ready?"

"Wait!" There was an awkward pause. "Could you just throw me a towel over the door first?"

"Oh. Of course." A fleecy blue towel was passed across the top of the shower frame.

Hastily Jennifer wrapped it around her slender body like a sarong. "Okay, say when."

"Now!" Seth ordered. He pulled with all his might while she pressed as forcefully as she could from the other side. In a split second the latch yielded and Jennifer came barreling through the open door right at Seth. He caught her as she fell.

"Sorry!" she exclaimed breathlessly as he steadied her in his arms. It was the second time in a week that the man had prevented her from landing rather painfully on a certain part of her anatomy.

"No need to apologize." Seth wasn't letting go, and he was staring at her intently.

Jennifer suddenly realized that the bath towel had come undone in the process, partially revealing one of her breasts. "Oh!"

Before she could do anything herself, Seth gently pulled the gaping ends of the towel back together, covering the perfect pink-tipped orb. "Don't be embarrassed," he urged in a soft, beguiling tone. "You're too beautiful to ever be embarrassed about anything."

"I'm dripping water all over you." Her voice was trembling.

"I don't care." Seth's hands moved up along the bareness of Jennifer's shoulders. "Your skin is like satin. Did you know that?"

"Seth?" She looked up at him questioningly. It was tantalizing being held like this. For a minute it seemed that he was about to kiss her.

His hands traveled down her arms. "You can drive a man crazy, Jennifer!" With a groan, he abruptly pulled away, oblivious to the fact that the entire front of his shirt and slacks was wet from the imprint of her body. Before she could utter a reply, Seth strode purposefully out of the room.

Chapter Seven

When Seth returned from his morning run early the next day, he informed Jennifer that after careful consideration he had decided to accept the chairmanship of the board of Ramsey Enterprises. Then, practically in the same breath, he told her that there was a benefit dinner dance at the Beverly Hilton that evening. How would she feel about coming with him? The way he asked, it almost seemed as if he half expected her to refuse. "I just happen to have a pair of tickets," came the explanation. "I buy them every year, but I've never actually gone."

"Sounds like it might be fun," she said, looking him directly in the eye. "I'd love to go."

"You would?"

"Sure, why not?" A dinner dance, Jennifer was thinking. It was bound to be one of those typical charity extravaganzas she had done her best to avoid most of her life. There would be the inevitable boring speeches and indifferent food, and someone at the table would be smoking the world's most offensive cigar. On the other hand, it provided the perfect opportunity to dance with her new husband. To be completely honest with herself, Jennifer thought, *that* was a tantalizing prospect. In fact, as long as she was being so truthful, it was something she had longed for over the past few days. She wanted this man to hold her and touch her. Embarrassment was not the only emotion Jennifer had experienced during that scene last night outside the shower.

"You don't think it will be too boring for you?"

Was that what he thought? "Perhaps," she said, trying to sound casual, "but it's the perfect opportunity to make a public appearance as an official married couple."

"Oh." He paused. "Of course." The smile left his eyes.

"About the corporation," Jennifer began, quickly changing the subject. "I'm glad you decided to take the position."

"Right, well, I'll get in touch with the lawyers. They'll draw up the necessary paperwork." There seemed to be something else Seth wanted to say.

"What time should I be ready tonight?"

"It starts at seven." He crossed his arms and looked at her quietly. "We can show up a little afterward."

"Fine."

"Jennifer, listen, if it gets too boring, we can always leave."

"I know." Somewhat belatedly it occurred to her that Seth was wearing gray sweatpants and a matching old sweatshirt with Harvard printed across the front. She hadn't realized until now what terrific physical shape the man was in. There was a lean, supple strength to his body, and unlike many men his age, Seth's stomach bore not even the slightest beginnings of a bulge. It was flat and hard. Goodness, what on earth was the matter with her? Jennifer was scandalized. Where were all these rebelliously sensual thoughts coming from, anyway? Oh, nonsense, another part of her conscience interjected assertively. There was absolutely nothing wrong with appreciating the male form. It was a perfectly natural thing, after all. Purely aesthetic. But there was nothing personal about it, of course. It wasn't as if she were falling in love with the man.

"Is something the matter?"

Jennifer coughed. "Certainly not." *In love with Seth Garrison, of all people?* Just because he was generous, understanding and sensitive? Just because he possessed that unique inner strength she had seen in only two other men in her entire life? Just because the way the man was looking at her right now turned her traitorous knees to jelly?

"So I'll see you around six-thirty," Seth was saying, completely oblivious to Jennifer's inner turmoil. Had he had any idea of the thoughts going on in his young bride's mind, his plans for the morning would have taken a radically different turn.

"*Right.*" She didn't say another word, merely watched him silently as he strode off to his room to shower and change. Her heart sank. This couldn't be possible. She couldn't be falling in love with Seth Garrison. After losing Kevin in that cruel way, Jennifer had promised herself she would never let it happen to her again. What she was experiencing now had to be an incredibly strong physical attraction—the natural female longing she had suppressed for so many years. It might be many things, but it certainly wasn't love. How silly! she thought, wanting to laugh. No one ever decided she was in love at eight o'clock in the morning, while standing next to a refrigerator, no less. These things simply didn't happen.

Later on that morning, Jennifer made several phone calls. The first she placed to the acting director of Ramsey Enterprises, informing him of her intention to name Seth as his replacement. The man, who was not particularly ambitious by nature, actually seemed pleased by the prospect of Seth Garrison as his successor. Next she called Professor Lovitt at the university, explaining that she would be delighted to accept the position as his teaching assistant starting in June. Finally, she called Anita.

"Well, well, if it isn't the newlywed. You're lucky you caught me," her friend declared. "I've got a very important interview at The Bistro in an hour."

"I'm really impressed. Listen, do you have an evening gown I can borrow?"

"Hmm, that's what I like. A friend I can't even impress with my incredible success."

"I already said I was impressed, didn't I?"

"Hmm. Nothing ever impresses you, Jennifer Ramsey," Anita said with feigned indignation. "Or should I say Jennifer *Garrison*. So, how's married life?"

"Different."

"How different?"

"Hey, are you going to lend me a dress or what?"

"Changing the subject, I see." Her friend sighed. "Yes, I've got five thousand dresses you can choose from. What's the occasion?"

"There's a fund-raiser at the Hilton—for quake relief."

"I heard about it. That's supposed to be an ultra-snazzy affair. Hey, you're actually going out formal, Jen! What am I saying? You're actually going out *period*. This ought to be declared a national holiday or something."

"Are you finished?" Jennifer pressed her lips together.

"Sure, for the moment. Now hop in that jalopy of yours and get over here. I have the perfect outfit for you."

"I don't want to make you late for your interview."

"Ah, don't worry. I'm a star, right? I'm supposed to show up late. It adds to my mystique."

Jennifer rolled her eyes. "Uh-huh."

A few minutes later she was driving along Sunset Boulevard toward the Pacific Coast Highway in Malibu. Despite its reputation for being a neon-lighted, bustling Hollywood thoroughfare, Sunset Boulevard became tranquil as it traveled westward through Beverly Hills, Jennifer thought. There it was a ribbon curving endlessly past lush green manicured lawns and a staggering sequence of spectacular homes. The road continued to climb, becoming less green and more rocky as she passed through the community of Pacific Palisades, a compatible blend of affluent homes and apartments—many perched high on the hillsides with stunning ocean vistas. Sunset Boulevard itself ended with a whimper, Jennifer mused, at the Pacific. All in all, thirty minutes had elapsed by the time she pulled her car into the tiny driveway alongside Anita's beach house. Had it been a warm, sunny summer day, the entire road would have been a noisy parking lot, jammed wall-to-wall with cars and sun worshippers and thousands of surfboards.

Anita was waiting in her bedroom with at least two dozen glittering gowns strewn carelessly across the bed. "Well, what do you think?" She held up a slinky little number in bright purple.

"That's a bit much," Jennifer said, smiling. "Where's the front of that dress, anyhow?"

"Hmm. Well, what about this one?"

"I'm going to a charity ball, not a police lineup."

Anita hesitated, then reached for a strapless jewel-toned green confection. "Okay, how's this? Sexy but classic."

There was no doubt about it, the dress was exquisitely made, by one of Hollywood's top theatrical designers. Although it was a bit revealing by Jennifer's standards, it was far less outrageous than the remaining selections sprawled across the comforter.

"Let me try it on," she conceded, figuring that with a string of pearls it would complete her appearance as a Beverly Hills matron.

"So," Anita murmured tentatively, "how's Seth?"

"Just fine." Jennifer unlaced her sneakers before stepping gingerly into the elegant satin gown. It seemed to fit perfectly.

"Very nice," Anita said with an approving nod, "but as I was saying, how's Seth?"

"I already told you, just fine." Jennifer zipped up the dress and studied her slender figure in the full-length mirror.

"It looks sensational. Wear it."

"That's the benefit of having a best friend with the exact same dress size."

"Yeah, yeah, so what's the story with the honeymoon?" Anita leveled a penetrating stare. "Did the two of you—"

"For heaven's sake, Anita!"

"Well, if the man is anything like his cousin . . ."

Jennifer quirked an eyebrow. "Are you saying that Daniel Garrison and you—"

"No, no." Anita waved her hand quickly. "But maybe I wouldn't have exactly objected. I mean, what a guy!"

"Excuse me, but what happened to Rod?"

"Rod *who*?"

"Oh, I see."

"Not that it matters," Anita said, flopping down on the mattress and crushing half a dozen expensive creations beneath her. "I thought Daniel was interested, but you know how it is." There was a wistful expression on her lovely face.

"So what happened?"

"Nothing happened, absolutely nothing at all! That's the problem. Men get intimidated by a celebrity, I guess. Anyhow, he never tried to kiss me or even ask for my phone number."

She looked so downcast that Jennifer offered, "I have an idea. Why don't I ask Seth—in a very subtle way—to let his cousin know that you're interested."

"No, absolutely not!"

"But if you really like the man—"

"Listen to me, Jen. A guy's got to be interested in a woman enough to want to make the first move. Call me old-fashioned, but it's something I happen to feel very strongly about."

"He does seem to be a very nice person, Anita," she said, pressing quietly. "A *real* man. How many of those do you have the opportunity to meet these days, especially in L.A.?"

"I don't care to pursue it." Anita was adamant. "If Mr. Daniel Garrison can't be bothered to pick up the telephone, then as far as I'm concerned, forget it. Besides—" she cleared her throat "—we were on the subject of you and Seth."

"What about me and Seth? We're just good friends."

"Gee whiz, I realize you've been out of circulation for a long time, but even with your limited experience with the opposite sex, surely you can tell when a man's interest in you is more than just friendly."

Jennifer felt a peculiar sensation in her stomach. "Anita, if you're attempting to make a point, I wish you'd go ahead."

"C'mon, kid, I was *there* Sunday. I saw the way he was looking at you. Never mind that, I saw the way he *kissed* you!"

"Oh, that." She shrugged. "We were just playacting for Charlotte's benefit."

"Yeah, right. It was a very convincing display. In fact, you convinced everybody in the entire restaurant."

"Good."

Anita narrowed her eyes speculatively. "You're nuts about the guy, aren't you?"

Jennifer almost choked. "Don't be ridiculous! I already told you it was all an act."

"You know, it's a funny thing about Seth Garrison. After all these years I realize he isn't half-bad. In fact, he turns out to be a real man, not one of those phonies. The guy is really okay. After the way we used to make his life miserable when we were kids. Go figure."

"Let me make this perfectly clear." Jennifer tossed the gown back on the bed. "I have no intention of becoming involved with Seth."

"You already *are* involved with him!"

"That's just for appearances, Anita."

"Hmm."

"Don't 'hmm.' You know very well that this marriage is in name only."

"Really," came the dry retort. "Well, allow me to put it this way, Jenni. If you don't watch your step, you might find yourself married in more than just *name only*!"

All that afternoon and early into the evening, Jennifer tried not to let Anita's warning disturb her. She even tried to convince herself that their main reason for attending this social event was to be seen by the Los Angeles establishment as a genuine married couple. But the thought of Seth's searing kiss on Sunday and last night's blatantly erotic incident in the bathroom made Jennifer shiver with delicious anticipation. She wanted Seth to hold her close again. She wanted to feel the sensual rhythm of the music as they danced together with their bodies touching. She wanted him to tell her once more that she was beautiful. She wanted—Jennifer stopped herself irritably. After all those years of numbness, the strong attraction that pulled her relentlessly toward Seth was a double-edged sword. She could allow herself, so very easily, to give in to this delectable sensation and follow with reckless abandon anywhere it might lead her.

On the other hand, there was such a bittersweet safety in being numb, completely invulnerable. There was a strong possibility that she might be letting herself in for rejection and pain.

Those thoughts troubled Jennifer deeply, and despite the fact that the late-afternoon chill was beginning to set in through the canyon, she stripped off her clothes, pulled on a bathing suit and slid open the glass doors of her bedroom. Stepping out onto the patio, she hesitated only a moment, feeling the cold wind against her face and legs. Then, with a furious determination, Jennifer dived into the deep end of the pool and swam twenty laps, hoping that enormous output of energy would clear her mind. It didn't.

All the resolutions Jennifer had made to herself fell by the wayside at seven o'clock that same evening. It was at that moment she opened the door to her bedroom, walked into the hallway and came face-to-face with Seth in a tuxedo.

"Jennifer!" He stopped adjusting a loose cuff link on his formal dress shirt and stared at her in mute admiration. His glittering blue eyes missed nothing, from the regal line of her nape revealed by the upswept hairstyle to the creamy rise of her naked shoulders above the strapless emerald satin of her dress. His gaze seemed to devour her as it continued downward, lingering at the deep cleft between her breasts. Revealed by the low-cut bodice, it evoked the tantalizing promise of what had been glimpsed on the previous evening. His eyes traveled lower to rest at the sweet curve of her hips outlined by the clinging material. "You're more lovely than I ever can begin to tell you," Seth uttered softly.

"Thank you." Jennifer had never felt so caressed by a man's gaze before. "You look rather handsome yourself."

"I doubt that." He twisted his lips wryly. "But I suppose I ought to thank you for the compliment, anyhow."

Why didn't he believe her, Jennifer thought in astonishment. Glasses and all, she had never seen a more attractive man. Seth Garrison was the perfect picture of worldly elegance and sophistication in his superbly fitting black tuxedo and matching slacks. How could she ever have doubted his incredible appeal? And how could *he* stand there and debate his own attractiveness? "I don't make insincere compliments."

He raised an eyebrow. "Well, let's just say you're being rather... generous in your praise."

"Rubbish. I don't say things I don't mean, Seth. The truth is, you look like someone out of *The Great Gatsby* or a Noël Coward play."

A muscle in his neck tensed. "Sure."

"Okay, but this is my last and final offer, Seth Garrison. How about a British secret agent?"

"Like James Bond?"

"Exactly." With those tortoiseshell rims and impeccable evening clothes, the man truly did resemble one of the dapper gentleman spies of popular fiction.

"Your credibility is slipping by the minute," came his dry observation.

The man truly refused to believe her, Jennifer thought. It was difficult to conceive of a man like Seth having such a negative opinion of his physical allure. It was strange to think of a person who appeared so confident as having such moments of insecurity. Amazing. "That's the last time I ever hand you a compliment!" she snapped in utter frustration.

Seth gave a resigned sigh, and they walked silently out to the car. They drove the brief journey to the hotel with a minimum of conversation. The lobby and grand ballroom were already jammed with guests when they arrived at the cocktail reception that preceded the dinner. From all over the Los Angeles area, the rich, the famous and the merely successful had shown up as part of the gala evening. The sequins on an endless parade of gowns glittered, incredible gems sparkled, and flashbulb after flashbulb exploded into tiny instants of blinding light. From everywhere, people approached who happened to know either Seth or Jennifer or both of them. The entire population of Beverly Hills seemed to give the couple their warmest congratulations on their sudden marriage.

"Why didn't you let us know?"

"What a surprise!"

"When did this happen?"

"You sly fox, Seth!"

"We had no idea you two were even dating!"

It went on and on like that for the rest of the evening, and after a while it grew rather tiresome. Most of the well-wishers were sincere in their comments, but all the knowing winks and ribald remarks caused Jennifer a good deal of embarrassment. Even Seth was visibly uncomfortable with some of the not-so-subtle innuendos.

"I'm sorry about this," he said quietly. "Perhaps coming here wasn't such a good idea."

"It's all right, really." Jennifer forced her most convincing smile. "Don't worry about it."

He shook his head in wonder. "You're a remarkable person, do you know that?"

"Now who's throwing out compliments?"

"I mean it, Jennifer. You never cease to amaze me." He reached out and took her hand in his, staring for a moment at the finger with the diamond ring and the wedding band. "I want you to know something else..." His voice was hoarse. "Something important to me—"

"Why, Seth Garrison! I've been looking all over for you!"

Whatever Seth had been about to say was forgotten as a robust middle-aged gentleman with steel-gray hair slapped him on the shoulder. "Oh." Seth adjusted his glasses. "Good evening, Martin."

The man grinned broadly and drew a cigar out of his jacket pocket. "I noticed from the arrangements that we'll be at the same table. . . ."

Terrific, Jennifer thought in dismay, envisioning an evening rife with pungent cigar fumes. With her luck, she would probably be sitting right next to the guy. Even before Seth had a chance to introduce them, she recognized him as Martin Crawley, one of the most prominent bankers in the city. His wife Mildred was a tight-lipped, bony woman with a deep bronze tan—the result of baking in Palms Springs sunshine for twenty years. She scarcely said a word all evening, except to the waiters. Other people at the table that night included a prominent television producer and his latest fiancée, several real-estate moguls and their wives and a celebrated Beverly Hills gynecologist with his actress girlfriend, both of whom chain-smoked during the entire meal.

The Ramsey name had always been quite impressive in social and business circles, especially in a town that worshiped money and power as fervently as Los Angeles did, Jennifer mused. Throughout her life, she had grown accustomed to the attention centered upon her at so many of these glittering charity affairs. All during the dinner she scarcely had an opportunity to exchange more than a few words with Seth. Her husband, already an important man in his own right, was constantly being asked for his opinion on one business matter or another. Now that word had begun to filter out that he was assuming the position of CEO of Ramsey Enterprises, his views and advice were considered more valuable than ever.

"Your husband is kind of cute," remarked the doctor's girlfriend confidingly, "for a guy with glasses."

"Thanks," Jennifer murmured, watching Seth out of the corner of her eye. He was calmly mediating a political dispute between the television producer and one of the real-estate tycoons. In the midst of a sentence he suddenly broke off what he was saying and smiled at her. A feeling of delicious warmth flooded Jennifer's body. She smiled back. Just at that moment the orchestra came back from its break and started to play "Moonlight Serenade."

"Excuse me," Seth said quietly. "I'd like to dance with my wife." He stood up and held out his hand, pulling Jennifer up from her chair in a single graceful motion. Silently he led her out onto the dance floor. "May I have this dance?" came the soft murmur.

Willingly Jennifer melted into his arms, placing one tentative hand on Seth's shoulder and allowing his own firm hand to grasp the other. For a few moments they danced that way, close but not intimate. They neither looked at each other nor exchanged a word of conversation. And then Jennifer found herself looking up at him. Their eyes suddenly locked. All at once she freed her hand from his gentle hold and brought it to rest along his other shoulder.

"Jennifer." Seth gave a broken sigh and pulled her tightly against him. Her face rested along the ruffled white silk of his shirt. The very scent of him was intoxicatingly male, a heady blend of his own body warmth and the musky cologne he wore.

Jennifer gave herself up to the exquisite pleasure of dancing with him. The classic strains of the ballad had a drugging quality. The two of them no longer really danced, but swayed back and forth slowly to the rhythm of the music. As they moved, Seth ran his hands up and down the bare skin of her back. He brought them to rest sensuously at the small of her back. Jennifer shuddered involuntarily at the underlying eroticism of the gesture.

"What is it?" Seth stared down at her questioningly, his voice practically a rasp.

"Nothing. Nothing at all," she murmured. "I had no idea you were such a good dancer."

"I assure you, it's the company I keep." His eyes narrowed. "Have I told you how beautiful you look this evening, Mrs. Garrison?"

Something in his tone made her quiver. "You don't look half-bad, yourself, Mr. Garrison." Jennifer managed the blithe reply, but her heart was pounding.

"We're just a mutual-admiration society, aren't we?"

"I suppose," she breathed against his chest.

"Oh, God!" Seth caught his breath and gazed down at her with a glitter in his eyes. "What am I going to do with you, honey?" He lowered his lips to her hair, bringing them in a maddeningly light motion toward the tender flesh of her earlobe.

"Seth." Jennifer swallowed convulsively. "What are you doing?"

He didn't answer for a moment. Completely occupied by the gentle kisses, his mouth was now teasing along the sensitive line of her nape.

"I'm crazy to do this," he finally uttered beneath his breath. "But I've just got to taste you, sweetheart."

His lips came down on hers in a soul-shattering kiss that rocked Jennifer to the very core of her being. All the inhibitions, all the fears, melted away in the path of this devastatingly sensual onslaught. It didn't matter that they were standing in the center of a crowded dance floor. It didn't matter that hundreds of people might be watching. All that mattered was that she was with Seth, being held by him and touched by him. How could she ever have denied her feelings for this wonderful man, feelings that crept up on her and caught her unawares? How could she have fought against her hunger for him, her need for something much more than mere friendship?

With an exultant sigh, Jennifer's lips parted beneath the tender urgency of his mouth. With a groan of astonishment mixed with pleasure, Seth sought out her moist sweetness. His tongue probed her inner secrets with piercing intensity, and shock waves rippled everywhere their bodies touched. He pressed her even more tightly against the lean, hard length of him, and then his hands moved from her slim back to mold the gentle curve of her hips.

"Do you have any idea what you're doing to me right now?" His voice was raw.

"What?" She ran her tongue over her lips in an unconsciously provocative gesture.

"This is definitely the wrong place to give you an answer to that, Jennifer."

"Where is the *right* place, then?"

He scorched her with the burning intensity of his gaze. "That's a very dangerous question to ask at the moment."

"Is that so?"

"Most definitely so, I assure you."

The orchestra's rendition of "Moonlight Serenade" came to an end, and the musicians segued into a fast-paced rock tune. Seth's arms dropped to his sides. "I'm a bit out of my element here," came the awkward confession. "Would you mind if we sat this one out?"

"I agree with you completely. Fast dancing is a major catastrophe where I'm concerned."

"I find that hard to believe."

"Why?"

"Because you've always been such a lively person. Lively people seem to have a natural affinity for the more upbeat music. Besides—" he paused "—back when you were a teenager, there were all those pool parties for your school friends—"

Jennifer threw her head back and gave an embarrassed exclamation. "Heavens, do you really remember those?"

"Of course."

The memories came flooding back to her. The impromptu get-togethers after class at the Ramsey estate in Bel Air. It was true that practically all of her schoolmates had had swimming pools of their own to frolic in, but it was also true that very few of them had had swimming pools or homes quite so spectacular as the one that Oliver Ramsey's millions had built. The real reason, however, that the Ramsey house had been a favorite hangout for Jennifer's classmates was the popularity of Jennifer herself. Though far too modest to ever admit it, she had been the best-liked person in her social circle. She had had a youthful magnetism and fun-loving spirit that made her the golden girl among her peers. With Anita as the adventurous sidekick and Kevin as her golden knight, the last few years of high school had been a delight.

Kevin. Strange, it no longer hurt to think about him anymore. He had been the son of a prominent Beverly Hills attorney and with dreams of following in his father's footsteps, he had a wonderful career ahead of him. Sweet, reckless Kevin—the captain of the football team, the most popular boy in the class.

But now, in retrospect, Jennifer could see that the love they had shared had been the first innocent stirrings of youth. An almost idealized version of the male-female relationship. At once it occurred to her that the tender passion between them might not have lasted with the passing years. No relationship could possibly be as picture-perfect as rose-hued memory tended to paint it.

"Is something wrong?"

Seth's concerned voice interrupted her thoughts.

"No, of course not. I was just—"

"Remembering?" he finished for her quietly.

"Well, yes."

"Those were happy days for you, weren't they?"

"Idyllic."

He touched her cheek with a sad smile. "I'm sorry I can't bring them back, Jennifer."

Impulsively she covered his hand with her own. "Perhaps those days belong where they are, in the past."

A muscle in his jaw tensed. "What are you trying to say?"

"That the past is over. The present is what matters." Jennifer lowered her lashes. "The present exists now. It has a life of its own."

There was a pause. "I suppose we should go back to our table."

"I suppose."

"Do you want to go back?"

She glanced over at the point in the distance where Martin Crawley was blowing columns of cigar smoke and the real-estate tycoons were arguing about tax shelters. "Not particularly. What about you?"

He nodded in agreement. "I second the motion. Let's get out of here."

Bestowing only the briefest of apologies and farewells upon their tablemates, the two of them retrieved Seth's Mercedes and were traveling up Benedict Canyon Drive moments later. It was a full moon that night, and the sky had an almost mystical glow. Neither of them spoke much during the short drive home. Seth seemed strangely preoccupied, and Jennifer had thoughts of her own.

Those teenage years had been rowdy and fun. Oliver Ramsey, as an indulgent single parent, had given in to his child's every whim. The pool parties that Seth had reminded her of had been noisy, and a bit silly, too. Rock music had blared from someone's portable cassette deck as Jennifer and her chums had tried to impress each other with the latest dance moves. Sooner or later everyone had ended up getting thrown in the enormous lagoon-style swimming pool. Only now could she remember the peripheral presence of Seth Garrison, wearing one of his somber suits, observing their youthful acrobatics from a distance.

"I suppose you thought we were spoiled, immature brats back then," she suddenly said aloud.

"I beg your pardon?"

"You know, during those boisterous after-school shindigs of mine."

"Actually, I didn't think that at all, Jennifer."

"You didn't?"

"No."

It was her turn to be confused. "What did you think, then?"

Seth kept his eyes on the road and said quietly, "I envied you."

"I don't understand."

He shrugged. "I won't bore you with any long stories. Suffice it to say that my own childhood was sadly lacking in exuberance." With that, he once again lapsed into silence for the rest of the ride.

There was an odd tension in the air between them, a tension that lay beneath all the casual conversation. It was an unspoken electrical charge that had existed ever since their passionate demonstration on the dance floor. It seemed as if each of them were waiting for the other to bring up the subject first. As far as Jennifer was concerned, it was painfully obvious that Seth once again regretted his impulsive actions. Probably, like her, he had misgivings about altering the delicate balance of their friendship. Fine, if that was the way he felt about the situation, far be it from her to force herself on the man. She wasn't dense, after all. She could take a hint.

When Seth pulled into the garage, he shut off the engine and turned to look at her. "I had a lovely time tonight."

Jennifer shrugged. "I'm thrilled." Without another word, she thrust the passenger door open and stalked toward the interior entryway. She heard another door slam behind her a few seconds later.

"Is something the matter?" came Seth's puzzled voice as he caught up with her.

"What on earth could possibly be the matter?" Jennifer crossed her arms disdainfully.

He quirked an eyebrow. "Are you mad at me for some reason?"

"Me, mad? I can't possibly imagine why, Mr. Seth Garrison!"

Dawning recognition spread across his gaunt face. "You *are* angry with me. What is it?"

"Forget it."

"Tell me what I did!" he demanded, grasping her shoulders. "Please tell me, Jennifer!"

"Well, here you are, a Harvard graduate—summa cum laude, no less—and you can't even figure out what's wrong!"

"No, I want you to tell me—" He stopped. "It's because I kissed you, isn't it?" Seth's fingers burned into her bare skin. "All right, I'm sorry, what else can I say? I lost my head!"

"I see," came the tight reply, "In other words, you're sorry it happened."

"No, I'm not sorry it happened. I'm apologizing for doing it. Do you understand the difference?"

"Why don't you explain it to me?"

He groaned. "I'm not responsible for my actions when I'm around you. That's the kind of effect you have on me, Jennifer." His hands moved down her back, traveling past the small of her back to her soft, rounded derriere. When he pressed her against the muscular hardness of his thighs, his legs positioned between hers made his frank arousal evidently clear. "I'm only human, honey. I want you so much it's tearing me up inside!"

Chapter Eight

Thrusting her aside, Seth fumbled for his house keys. In another moment he stalked through the kitchen and into the spacious living room, with Jennifer close behind him. Clearly agitated, he turned to face her at last. "I thought I could do it, Jennifer, but this so-called arrangement of ours just isn't going to work."

"Do you mean—"

His jaw tightened. "No, it's not what you think. I mean to stand by you on the matter of Oliver's will, but we can't live together anymore."

Jennifer's heart sank. "You want me to leave?"

"Hell, no! That's the problem," he ground out. "I want you here, but I can't allow you to stay. Go back to your own apartment, and if people talk, well, let them! Being under the same roof like this is out of the question!''

"Why?" She sounded almost plaintive, and it touched Seth's heart.

"Because we're supposed to be just friends, and I can't be just friends with you. I want more than that."

"Oh." An indescribable warmth flooded through her.

"Do you understand now?" came his painful retort. "Something has to be done. I can't go on this way any longer."

"I agree."

"Then it's decided." Seth's tone was husky and faraway. "I'll help you move out whenever you want—"

"That's not what I agree about. The truth is—" Jennifer gazed up at him shyly "—I don't want to be just friends, either."

A strange light came into his silver-blue eyes. "What is it you're telling me?"

"I don't want to leave, Seth. Please don't ask me to go." She pressed her hand against the front of his shirt.

"Don't play with me, Jennifer," he warned.

"I'm not playing." In an attempt to convince him, she daringly wrapped her arms around his neck and, standing on tiptoe, pressed her lips against his hard mouth.

Drawing away after a moment, he stared at her in utter astonishment. "Do you know what you're doing? Don't you realize what something like this can lead to?''

In mute understanding, Jennifer planted delicate butterfly kisses along the taut line of his jaw, down toward the tense cord of his throat. All the years of holding back, all the unfulfilled needs of her vital womanhood, pushed her over the brink of boldness. It seemed Jennifer had waited forever to feel like this. Her frustrating, furtive necking sessions with Kevin had aroused her desires, but nothing Kevin and she had shared had borne the incredible emotional impact of this moment alone with Seth in his living room.

''You're playing with fire,'' Seth growled before taking her face in his hands and kissing her hungrily. He pressed his lips to her cheeks, her forehead, her eyelids, then took her mouth with an almost desperate urgency. Jennifer strained to get even closer, and Seth gave a visible shudder as her breasts pressed against the thin material of his ruffled shirt. ''I want you so badly I'm going out of my mind!'' Ruthlessly his mouth continued to ravage her own, making way for the plundering of his tongue. Then, all at once, his hands grasped her waist, and he pulled his lips from hers to burn a trail of liquid fire down her throat and beyond, toward the shadowy cleft between her breasts.

How long they stood locked in that heated embrace, Jennifer couldn't tell. Vaguely, in some remote corner of her mind, she was aware of being lifted up in Seth's arms and carried over to the leather sofa.

And then he lowered her tenderly against the cushions.

"Do you know how much I've wanted this?" came his rough whisper. He appeared to tower over her for a moment, as if deeply disturbed by a sudden thought. Jennifer's hair was loose now, spilling around her flushed face like a silken cloud. She gazed up at Seth mutely, dizzy from his overwhelming display of passion. She had no way of knowing that with her hazel eyes glowing and the snug green satin bodice revealing the rapid rise and fall of her breasts, she was inciting Seth to near-madness.

He had dreamed of this—the woman he desired more than any other in the world lying stretched out beneath him on a couch, her hair a golden tangle, her lips still moist from his kisses. He knew it was wrong, it was careless—hell, it was downright irresponsible—but he had to have her now. All the promises Seth had made to himself were forgotten tonight. Call him a fool to rush her, but he couldn't wait any longer for Jennifer to be his woman in the truest sense of the word. Even though he realized that what she felt for him was simple desire, not love, he would settle for that. He would settle for anything this delectable creature was willing to give him. For it was not much more than a mere week ago that to even *hold* Jennifer Ramsey had seemed like the very height of improbability. He sighed. Tonight that time might well have been somewhere in the distant past. Fighting his conscience every step of the way, Seth determined to make her want him as badly as he wanted her. He silently vowed to make her forget any other man. It was ruthless and perhaps even heartless, but he would not be satisfied until all thoughts of Kevin Stern were driven from her mind by the sheer persuasive power of his lovemaking.

He tugged off his tuxedo jacket impatiently, letting it drop to the floor in a crumpled, expensive heap. Then just as recklessly, he tossed his eyeglasses over on the chrome coffee table and at long last lowered himself onto the couch. With another sigh he gathered Jennifer in his arms and continued the seduction.

What on earth was she doing, Jennifer thought, trembling in Seth's passionate embrace. She was behaving like a wild, reckless woman who had thrown all caution to the wind. "Kiss me, Seth!" She actually heard the brazen words from her own lips.

"I'll kiss you as much as you want, sweetheart," he uttered thickly. "I'll kiss you all over, until you tell me to stop!" His mouth was at once hot and sweet, plucking the nectar from her lips until he had drunk his fill of her heady wine. He probed, he tasted, he planted maddening caresses along her nape. But he had only begun his ruthlessly sensual battle for the ultimate possession. "Do you like it when I do this?" He nibbled the sensitive flesh of her earlobe. "Tell me you like it, honey!"

Jennifer gave a moan. "Oh, yes! Oh—" She shut her eyes convulsively. She was being seduced in the most superb, most expert fashion. She knew, and she

didn't care. It was enough just to give herself up to the
erotic pleasure of being savored by this man who just
happened to be her husband.

Then his hands grew bolder, moving toward the
zipper at the back of her evening dress. With a single,
swift motion, Seth unfastened it halfway. Hesitating
only for a few seconds, he gently pulled the front of
the gown to the waist, exposing her perfect breasts to
his hungry gaze.

"Seth!" she gasped, simultaneously shocked and
thrilled.

His eyes glimmered with raw passion. "You're incredibly beautiful, do you know that?" One of his
hands reached out to cup an exquisite orb. "I've
dreamed of touching you this way! You're like silk in
my hands, Jennifer!" In a shattering gesture, he bent
his head down and pressed his mouth to one pink nipple, teasing it to hardness.

"What...oh, what are you doing?" Jennifer's voice
was scarcely audible.

"I'm touching you, darling. Tell me you don't like
it and I swear I'll stop!"

How could she ask him to stop, Jennifer wanted to
cry out. He was pulling her deeper and deeper into a
hypnotic whirl of sensation. His hands stroked and
caressed her breasts with possessive boldness, inciting
her to helpless shivers of delight. She only wanted to
feel and keep on feeling his touch all over. "No," she
moaned breathlessly. "Don't stop, Seth. Please!"

"I've just begun," he rasped as his tongue darted out to taunt her tender skin until her entire body shook from the intensity of it. She was on fire for him, being driven to the brink of madness by his tongue, his mouth, his firm, knowing hands.

Then his own breathing became ragged, and with darkened eyes he rolled completely on top of her with a strange new urgency. She was completely a captive of his hard, muscular strength, trapped beneath Seth's powerful arms and thighs. And there, unmistakably, was the evidence of his male arousal. "Can you feel what you're doing to me, honey? Can you tell how much I want you?" It was not just his voice trembling now, but his entire body. It gave Jennifer an unbelievable feeling of power...that unexpectedly delicious realization that she could do this to him, make him lose control in such a devastating and erotic way. Who would ever have believed that such vulnerability lay just beneath the surface of this man? A tenderness no one could possibly have guessed existed beneath Seth Garrison's cool, businesslike exterior. She would follow wherever he was going to lead her, a joyful, willing disciple to his masterful lovemaking.

How long they lay together, locked in the preliminary throes of passion, there was no way of knowing. It might have been minutes, and it might have been hours. Time as Jennifer had come to understand it stood still as she was consumed by a maelstrom of sensation. Seth was utterly enveloping her in kisses and intimate caresses over her mouth, her neck, her breasts, and now his heated lips were searing their unique brand down toward her supple stomach. He loosened the back zipper of the green silk gown, urging it impatiently toward her hips. "You looked so damn sexy in this little dress tonight," came the thick whisper. "All I could think about was peeling it off you." His firm, hard hands guided the flimsy satin material down past the smooth columns of her thighs, past her knees, then pulled it impatiently away from her body. The expensive designer creation fell to the carpet, crumpled in a forgotten heap, where it was destined to remain until it was discovered there the next morning.

"Every inch of you is exquisite." His eyes devoured the newly exposed flesh. "Just as I imagined it would be!" She was naked beneath him except for her pink silk bikini panties, which only enflamed his senses even more.

"Seth," she murmured breathily, "maybe we shouldn't—"

"No, honey." Her husband positioned himself between her nearly bare hips and began to move against her in a startlingly explicit new way. "We *should*!"

"But . . ." Jennifer tried to ignore the burning demands of his tongue as it flickered back and forth across one pink-tinged nipple. It was impossible to concentrate on what she wanted to say. "But," she repeated in fitful gasps, "I feel so . . . so out of control!"

"It's supposed to feel that way, sweetheart, don't you know that?" His breathing grew even heavier now, and he gazed down at her lovingly. "Crazy, reckless, spiraling out of control!" With unbelievable tenderness, he brushed back the wild, silken strands of blond hair from her forehead. "How could I have ever imagined it could be like this, though?" Seth didn't wait for an answer, but reached for his dress tie and unfastened it urgently, throwing the scrap of black silk down to join the satin gown on the plush carpet. Hastily he ripped open the buttons of his ruffled shirt, exposing the taut, muscled flesh of his chest. A narrow pelt of dark hair was revealed to the waist, and the impact was even more disturbingly masculine than Jennifer thought possible.

"I want to feel your skin against mine," he uttered raggedly. "You're sweet satin to my touch!"

When his naked skin came in contact with Jennifer's breasts, she knew there was no way to resist the aching drive toward fulfillment. She loved this man. He had slowly crept into her heart, unseen and unsuspected. His skillful caresses were urging her to madness, steering both body and mind upward, higher and higher, in a dizzying spiral.

"Do you want me, my love?" he demanded hotly. "Do you want me now?"

Jennifer swallowed convulsively. "Yes."

"Then say the words," came the hoarse plea. "I need to hear you tell me!"

"Yes, I want you, Seth!" she whispered with a shudder. "I want you to make love to me, now!"

"Yes, sweetheart." Strong arms lifted her up from the couch, cradling her against his bare chest. "I'll make love to you, but not here. The first time I make you mine won't be stolen moments on a living-room sofa." With a groan, Seth moved toward the hallway, carrying Jennifer into the shadowy coolness of his bedroom. Then she was being gently deposited on the down-covered mattress. Pausing just long enough to remove his trousers, he slid into bed beside her. Tenderly he kissed her mouth and reached down to touch the lacy waistband of her panties.

Seth could actually feel the red-hot rush of blood to his head. Inside, he was shaking. For years he had dreamed of such a moment with Jennifer, vainly attempting to imagine what it would be like. And now reality was outdoing every fantasy Seth had ever experienced. But deep in the back of his mind a warning bell went off. He was breaking every resolution he had made to himself. Here was Jennifer, lying beneath him, looking up at him with those beautiful, bright hazel eyes. God, how he wanted her right now. But the warning bell kept growing louder and louder. It would take every ounce of willpower to keep the promise he had made to himself when this charade had begun, but in his troubled heart Seth knew he had no choice. If he made love to her now the way he ached to do, later he would be forced to pay the price for his foolishness. Jennifer would only hate him later. For her this wasn't real. It was only a moment of madness.

Seth stopped unexpectedly, pulling away from her with a groan. "No. This is wrong."

"Seth?" She looked up at him in confusion.

"I can't do this," came the harsh exclamation. "It isn't right." Abruptly he reached for his trousers and drew them back on. Without another word he placed a soft velour robe around Jennifer's nude body. "Go to bed, Jennifer. Back to your *own* bed."

"What's the matter?" Her voice was filled with hurt and disbelief. "What have I done?"

"You haven't done anything, honey," he said, shaking his head bitterly. "It's all my fault."

"I don't understand—" She sounded so lost and alone that Seth wanted to fold her in his arms again and tell her it was all a misunderstanding, but he couldn't. He had to give her more time. It was the only way to not risk losing her trust. And maybe one day she might even learn to love him, but that fantasy seemed too much to hope for.

"It's hard to explain," Seth began shakily, guiding his bride back to her own bedroom. "But if I make love to you now, the way I'm aching to do, it would be taking unfair advantage of the situation." Desperately he tried to ignore the tantalizing expanse of creamy flesh exposed through the gap in Jennifer's borrowed robe.

Her lips tightened as she stood in the hallway with him. "Is that what you think? That you'd be taking advantage of me?"

"You're very... vulnerable right now."

"Is that what you think?" Her hazel eyes were luminously expressive.

"Oh, God!" he groaned. "Don't look at me like that."

"Like what?" Jennifer was at a loss to comprehend his sudden rejection. "How can you play these games with me, Seth?"

"Games? I'm not playing any games with you, honey. The stakes in this are too damn high!"

This was the man who had trembled with passion in her arms just moments before, and now he had unceremoniously thrust her away. In her entire life Jennifer had never begged any man to make love to her, and despite her tumult of feelings she had too much pride to ask Seth now. But something in her traitorous heart sought an answer, a kind of reconciliation. "Seth..." She reached out to touch his face.

He flinched as if he had just been stung. "No," came the anguished command. "Go to bed, Jennifer. Go while I can still let you!" With a tortured oath, he turned on his heel and strode stiffly down the darkened corridor. He never even turned back once, but disappeared into his own room, slamming the door shut behind him.

Chapter Nine

The following morning, Jennifer lay huddled beneath the covers of her bed, lost in the swirling confusion of her thoughts.

Contrary to popular belief, it was possible to grow up in Beverly Hills and have a perfectly normal, happy childhood, she thought. Jennifer still sent Valentine Day cards to her old elementary school chums and never forgot a birthday. The friends she had made at an early age were, with few exceptions, the ones she had kept. As a rule, they were all children of important people. Sometimes, as in the case of Kevin, the parents were rich but not famous, and occasionally, as in the case of Anita Bailey, the parents were famous but not very rich. But whatever the particular combination was, it didn't matter. What Jennifer and her friends learned quickly in life was that there would always be those people who would be nice to them because of who their parents were. Consequently, Jennifer had developed unfailing instincts where human nature was concerned. She possessed an uncanny ability to detect when a person was being manipulative or insincere. The first time she had been introduced to Charlotte DeLeon, for example, Jennifer had immediately sensed the vicious side of her stepmother's character and had always taken care to be on her guard to avoid a confrontation.

On the other hand, she had known from the very moment she'd met Seth Garrison that he was a man to be trusted. Even as a youngster she had been perceptive enough to recognize the sterling qualities of honesty and fair play.

It was those qualities, Jennifer was convinced, that had caused his sudden rejection of her just as they had been about to make love. After the initial confusion, hurt and bruised pride had passed, she had realized that in a stunning way, Seth's abrupt departure demonstrated those very strengths of character that she had come to admire in the man. In his mistaken but well-meaning view, he actually believed he had done the right and noble thing. Completely misconstruing the situation, he thought Jennifer had turned to him out of vulnerability and blind need. Because of the kind of man Seth was, his conscience couldn't permit the final consummation. His attitude was the closest thing to chivalry that Jennifer had ever seen. In Seth's own touchingly old-fashioned way, he was trying to protect her from herself.

What he didn't realize, though, was that Jennifer did not need or even *want* that protection. Her actions last night had had nothing at all to do with weakness or vulnerability. What Jennifer had felt for him last night was love, pure and simple. Somewhat belatedly she understood that there was no way Seth could be aware of the true depth of her emotions. She had said nothing that might even remotely have given the man a clue to her true feelings for him. The most difficult thing for a woman to do was to tell a man she was in love with him before he confessed to being in love with her. This is a matter of simple female pride, a rule that only the most hasty and unwise would venture to break.

Words of love did not come easily to Jennifer's lips. In her entire life she had only declared those words to one other man, and that had been Kevin. And now, at long last, once again she had managed to find someone wonderful, but she dared not risk such a confession yet. In truth, Jennifer might not ever tell Seth she was in love with him. If it happened that his feelings for her were not the same, then she would have spared herself an embarrassing moment. But nothing now was going to prevent Jennifer from showing him, without words, her love. She felt no shame or even shyness about her plan of action. Seth Garrison was the man who had unexpectedly guided her out of the dark limbo in which she had existed for years and magically made her life whole again.

Jennifer wanted to laugh and cry at the same time. She had never felt so alive, so full of joyful optimism. The world was bright and shiny again, as it had been when she had been a child. In little more than a week's time, one person had made all the difference and had changed her entire outlook. It was an open question whether or not Seth loved her, but his intense physical hunger for Jennifer was one thing that could not be disputed. And he cared for her as a person—she knew that, as well. In the meantime, Jennifer would not even bring up the subject of love. Right now all she intended to do was wear down the man's resistance. And maybe then, if she was lucky, he would wake up one morning to discover that she had crept into his heart the same way he had unwittingly crept into hers.

Seth left the house before Jennifer awakened that morning. It was quite obvious to her that he wanted to avoid a confrontation about the incident of the night before. At this point, Jennifer believed she could read him like a book. It didn't take a rocket scientist to figure out that the man was both embarrassed and remorseful. Strangely, he didn't seem to blame her in any way for the situation, and that proved how incredibly old-fashioned Mr. Seth Garrison was. But Jennifer had plans of her own. She would show him that there was absolutely nothing to be embarrassed or remorseful about. There was no law that said a man couldn't seduce his own wife, after all. But if need be she would show Seth that the reverse was also true. There was surely nothing scandalous about a wife wanting to seduce her own husband.

All during the day Jennifer tried to distract herself by running a series of minor errands. She went to her favorite Hollywood car wash and had her beloved red Mustang hot-waxed. She drove down to the Farmers' Market to buy a bag of tangerines. She paid a visit to several family acquaintances and broke the news of her marriage. She then told each of them to put her name back on the active fund-raiser list of any charitable organization they happened to run. She was met with both astonishment and delight. Yes, Jennifer thought later, smiling to herself, welcome back to the world of the living. She felt involved and alive again.

Jennifer drove down Santa Monica Boulevard with a contented expression on her face. But instead of turning north when she reached the light at Beverly Drive she made a left turn toward the popular shopping area known as the golden triangle in Beverly Hills. Located on those few blocks were the most exclusive stores in the entire world. It was also one of the few places anywhere that there was free municipal valet parking. On impulse, Jennifer left her car with one of the attendants in the public lot and took a leisurely stroll down Brighton Way and then onto famous Rodeo Drive. As she passed one of the many jewelry stores, her eye was caught by a simple but elegant gold tie bar. In the center was a single diamond, yet the piece was in no way flashy or ostentatious. Jennifer couldn't help but grin to herself. For a man like Seth, who always wore a suit and tie, this was the perfect accessory.

She wondered what his reaction would be if she were to buy it for him as a gift. Well, the truth was she hadn't given him a single present during their marriage, and after all, he had given her that spectacular diamond solitaire. Jennifer decided she wanted to give her husband a present. It was fitting and right.

When she went inside the jeweler's shop, the gentleman who waited on her politely asked, "Is this for a special person?"

Jennifer smiled back and answered softly, "Yes, a very special person. My *husband*."

When she returned home, she found a halting, awkward message on the answering machine from Seth, informing her that he would be working very late and had no idea when he was coming home. Although Jennifer bit her lip in disappointment, Seth's behavior didn't surprise her. She had expected him to go out of his way to avoid her.

But sooner or later he would have to leave the safety of his office and venture back to the house in Benedict Canyon. No matter how late he was going to be, Jennifer had every intention of waiting up for him. She gazed out the huge living-room window at the setting sun. Though she was unaware of it, a smile crept across her face.

When the phone suddenly rang, Jennifer raced for it, tripping over a chair and crashing headlong into the sofa. Limping painfully to pick up the receiver, she shook her head in resignation. Certain things would never change, Jennifer supposed. She would probably always be the same accident-prone creature she had been since birth. It was her belief that all furniture, doorknobs and staircases had been put on this earth for the sole purpose of creating her personal obstacle course. She lifted the telephone to her ear, secretly hoping it was Seth. "Hello?"

"Hey, you're home!" A familiar voice sparkled on the other end. "Boy, have I got some gossip for you!"

"Oh, Anita. How are you?" She tried to conceal her disappointment.

"That's what I wanted to tell you. He called!"

"Who called?"

"Wendell Wynberg!"

"The movie director?"

"He's taking me out to dinner, can you believe it? I'm so excited I can't stand it!" Anita babbled.

"That was quick. So what happened to your mad crush on Daniel Garrison?"

"Daniel *who*?"

Jennifer rolled her eyes. "I have the strangest feeling we've had this conversation before."

"No, you don't understand, dummy. This isn't a date. Wendell wants to talk about casting me for the lead in that picture!"

No one had to ask what "that picture" was, of course. The novel *Enchanted Galaxies* had been a runaway bestseller since its publication two years ago. There had been feverish bidding throughout Hollywood for the screen rights to the fantasy-romance blockbuster. In the end it was the roly-poly wunderkind himself, Wendell Wynberg, who had walked off with the prize. Still in his thirties, the young genius had become the most successful producer-director in the history of motion pictures, with a special place in his heart for science fiction and high adventure.

"That's fabulous news, Anita. Congratulations!"

She sighed. "I still can't get over it. Every actress in town has been trying to win the part. The talk is that our beloved Charlotte even offered to pay Wendell five million dollars if he signed her for the role!"

"Very interesting." Now it was starting to make sense. How could she have underestimated her stepmother's colossal ego? She wanted to be able to buy her way into any film she desired. No wonder her greed over the will was bottomless, Jennifer thought.

"Anyway, I was wondering how things were going with you and Seth."

"Fine."

"Details, I want details!" the young actress pleaded.

"Please don't start embarrassing me."

"Oh, listen! I'm her best friend, and now I'm embarrassing her!"

"Seriously, Anita. I'd rather not talk about it."

"I'm waiting," came the imperious demand from the other end of the telephone line. "If you don't tell me all the intrigue this minute, then you're an insensitive and heartless human being and you can certainly forget the wonderful Christmas present I was going to get for you!"

"Christmas isn't for another eight months."

"That's far enough for me to forget it! C'mon, Jen, I've waited seven years to hear some *real* gossip from you! Don't I always tell you all of mine?"

Jennifer sighed resignedly. What was the point of trying to keep secrets from Anita Bailey, of all people? Sooner or later her ebullient childhood friend would find out anyway. Slowly, with some substantial editing in the more sensitive spots, she told of the romantic encounter that had flared into being the previous evening. She described how Seth had put the brakes on suddenly and told of his apparently bittersweet regret.

After Anita had finished listening, she asked quietly, "Do you love him?"

Jennifer drew a breath. "Yes, I do." The words were out now. She had confessed her feelings openly, even if only to an old friend.

"Then I think you should tell him what you feel. Tell Seth that you love him."

"I won't do that," she retorted. "I have no desire to make a fool of myself, Anita."

"How could you possibly be making a fool of yourself? The guy is nuts about you!"

"That remains to be seen."

"Oh, please! You must be blind *and* dumb not to know what everyone else in the world seems to know, except you."

"I'm not telling Seth Garrison anything. What if he isn't interested in me the same way—"

"Exactly how stupid *are* you?"

Jennifer bit her lip. "I'm serious, Anita. I happen to have a few remaining ounces of pride."

"Yeah, well, pride goeth before a fall," the voice on the other end of the telephone line declared. "Don't say I didn't warn you."

Seth didn't return home until much later that night. Jennifer could no longer keep her eyes open, so she took the wedding gift and left it on his bed, feeling that the small card reading Grooms deserve presents, too, was explanation enough.

Wearily she went back to her own room and undressed. After slipping on a nightgown she pulled back the covers and got into bed.

A few minutes later she was fast asleep. She didn't hear his car as it entered the garage. A short time later, she was completely unaware of the knock on her bedroom door. Jennifer slept on as his voice gently called out her name. It wasn't until a hand touched her shoulder and someone's weight compressed a spot next to her on the mattress that she awoke to see Seth sitting alongside her in the dim light of her room.

"Jennifer," he whispered urgently.

With slow surprise, she opened her drowsy eyelids. "Seth. What are you doing here?"

"I wanted to talk to you."

Alertness began flooding back to her. Pausing to brush the stray wisps of hair from her eyes, Jennifer reached out and turned on the lamp. Her eyes took a moment to get accustomed to the sudden brightness. During that time, she grew aware of Seth just sitting there, watching her in silence. She yawned involuntarily. "What did you want to talk about?"

"This." He held the gold-and-diamond tie bar in his hand.

"Oh, that. It's not too loud, is it?"

"Jennifer..." His voice was hushed. "Why did you buy it for me?"

"I thought it was obvious. A wedding present."

"After the way I treated you last night, you went out and got me a wedding present?" He sounded incredulous. "A piece of jewelry that, I might add, must be outrageously expensive."

"Oh, please. If you really want to talk about something outrageously expensive, let's talk about the piece of jewelry you bought *me*, Seth Garrison!"

"That was different," he retorted harshly.

"This should be interesting. Tell me why it was different." Jennifer propped herself up in bed, unconscious of the allure of her skimpy nightgown.

Seth stared at the thin nylon material, which clearly outlined her breasts, and at the narrow pink spaghetti straps, which did little to conceal her creamy skin. He coughed. "I just don't understand why you would spend so much money on me."

"I can spend all the money I want. I *am* rich, as you probably are aware." She smiled in spite of herself. "Honestly, I cannot imagine why you're making such a fuss about this. I thought it was perfectly natural for a woman to buy her husband an occasional gift. I saw it in a shop window this afternoon and immediately thought of you."

A silver light suddenly flickered in his eyes. "You thought of me?" he murmured.

"How could anyone see a tie bar and not think of the man of a thousand suits and ties?" Her reply was deliberately casual.

"Is that what you call me?"

"Well . . ." She hesitated. "You do seem to have a lot of suits."

He twisted his lips. "How do you know I don't just keep wearing the same one over and over?"

What is going on, Jennifer wondered. Were they actually sitting on her bed in the middle of the night discussing the stimulating topic of a man's wardrobe? Or was this conversation really about something else? Despite her slightly groggy state, there was no missing the underlying air of tension between them. "If you don't like the tie bar, that's another subject entirely. The jeweler said he'd be happy to exchange it for something else. Perhaps you'd rather have a nice pair of cuff links."

"Jennifer, I really like the gift. It was very generous of you. I just feel strange about accepting—"

She folded her arms abruptly. "Here's the deal, Mr. Garrison. If I can accept *your* present, then you have to accept *my* present. Fair is fair. I needn't remind you of the Marquis of Queensberry rules."

His mouth twitched. "Jennifer, you're so disarming. I never know what to expect next from you."

"That ought to make us about even. I never know quite what's going to come next with you, either."

There was a long silence. "About last night—"

"Forget it," she said nervously.

"But I don't want to forget about it, honey. I don't want to forget anything that happened between us." Seth moved toward her slowly. "I've felt damn rotten all day long about it."

Out of nowhere, a pillow landed squarely on top of his head. "What the—"

"That's for having the nerve to actually apologize for last night! Of all the insulting, outrageous things to do—"

"I don't understand this at all, Jennifer. I'm simply trying to explain my behavior last night. I lost control, I confess that freely. I promise it won't happen again—" Another pillow smacked down on his perfectly arranged hair. "What was *that* one for?" he inquired coldly.

"I agree your behavior was disgraceful, Seth, but not for the reason you think. What I object to is a grown man who acts like a tease."

"What?"

"Just what I said, a tease." Jennifer could not believe that her tongue could be this reckless.

A muscle throbbed in his taut neck. "I wasn't teasing you last night, Jennifer. You should know that."

"I don't know anything of the kind." She lowered her eyes to stare blindly at the down comforter. "I only know that last night you made me feel things I thought I would never—" She stopped abruptly, aware of his incredulous stare. "The point is, you made me want to—"

"I made you want to *what*?" he asked quietly.

"Make love with you."

"I lost my head last night, but can you blame me? You looked so damn beautiful I couldn't stop myself." His eyes narrowed. "You drove me crazy, just the way you're driving me crazy this minute!" With a groan, he pulled her into his arms roughly. "Just let me touch you, sweetheart. I promise I won't do anything to hurt you!" His hungry mouth sought out the sweetness of her own, and his hands pressed possessively against the small of Jennifer's back.

With joyous relief, she clung to him, her willing arms twining happily around his neck. "You can't hurt me!'' she whispered between his drugging kisses. *Because I love you!*

His fingers slid traitorously underneath the thin straps of her nightie. ''You're all silk and honey, did you know that?'' The straps fell down past her shoulders, causing the pink bodice to slip even lower, revealing the pink tips of her breasts. ''Just look at you.'' His tone was husky. ''What am I supposed to do? I'm only human.'' His hard fingers pulled the flimsy material all the way down to Jennifer's waist. With infinite tenderness, he caressed each nipple to hardness before fastening his mouth over one of the perfect nubs. His tongue flickered maddeningly, just as it had the night before, across the sensitive, velvety skin. And then he was carrying her back down with him against the pillows, touching her everywhere and endlessly.

''Your glasses are all fogged up,'' she breathed.

''To hell with my glasses,'' Seth said, tossing them onto the floor, ''and to hell with my good intentions!'' He had to have been a fool last night not to have taken what Jennifer had so freely offered. And now that he was in paradise again, Seth was determined not to make the same mistake twice. Not with Jennifer lying beneath him so provocatively, practically naked. She was the woman he had adored from afar for years, and here she was pressed up against him, so sweet and so unbelievably willing! Tearing himself away from her satin embrace last night had been the most difficult thing he had done in his entire life. He'd turned away from the delicious promise of indescribable pleasure and let her walk back to her room, leaving him cold and empty. His reasoning had been not to take advantage of a woman's moment of weakness, but why had he insisted on being so damn noble? What if Jennifer could never fall in love with him? What if when the year was out she left his life forever and met a man she truly wanted? What would he have gained by pushing her away? Why should he be a hero, anyhow? If he were ruthlessly honest with himself, Seth confessed, he wanted Jennifer whether she cared for him or not. Even if all she felt for him was natural human desire, he didn't care anymore. He wanted her so desperately that he was willing to take her on any terms.

Jennifer, too, was lost in a mad frenzy of desire. She was even more aroused than she had been the night before. She suddenly realized that this time it was going to happen. By the way Seth looked at her now, his body trembling and his pupils dilated with passion, she knew with delicious certainty that he had no intention of stopping himself this time. Almost savagely, his fingers pulled the nightdress away from her slender body, exposing her complete nakedness to his hungry gaze.

"You're so perfect," he uttered thickly, "so incredibly exquisite!" In a moment he was tearing away his own clothes, and then there was no barrier between them but skin against skin.

"Seth!" she gasped as she felt his unrestrained male arousal for the first time.

"You should stop me!" he said in a final raw plea.

"I can't," Jennifer confessed, on fire for him. She arched her body up to his, no longer afraid or unsure. This was what she had always wanted, what she had waited for.

I'm not asking you to love me, Seth begged silently. *Just care a little, my lovely Jennifer! Because it means so much to me. It's got to be more than just sex.*

But Jennifer was completely unaware of his inner turmoil. The fire raging beyond the privacy of each of their thoughts was burning out of control now.

"Tell me this is what you want, too!" he ground out. "Tell me you won't change your mind, sweetheart!"

"I want you, Seth!" she responded with breathless urgency.

It was doubtful that Seth could have stopped himself now even if he had wanted to. He smoothed the silky skin of her thighs with gentle but firm caresses, guiding his own legs between them. As he moved above her slowly, his eyes never left her face. "Are you sure, my sweet Jennifer? Are you really sure?"

She looked up at him mutely and nodded, allowing her hands the thrill of touching his taut chest. "Yes, please!" she finally said.

He began to move against her in an entirely new way. This was far more erotic, far more intimate.

There was a sharp pain, and she cried out involuntarily.

"Jennifer!" Seth stared down at her in total shock. "But this can't be possible. . . . You can't be!"

But her pain disappeared as quickly as it had come.

In all his wild imaginings, Seth had never considered that Jennifer could still be a virgin! Surely she had made love with her fiancé. If not, then there must have been someone to answer her desires during the past seven years. She was beautiful and sexy. How could she possibly have remained untouched for so long? But despite his self-recriminations, Seth could not stop making love to this exquisite creature.

For Jennifer, the pain was slowly replaced by something so astonishing and intensely delightful that she could not believe such sensations existed. All of a sudden she was crying from the sweet pleasure of it as Seth drew her even more tightly against the lean, hard length of him, driving them both to an inevitable, shattering fulfillment.

Chapter Ten

Dammit, Jennifer, you should have told me!" Seth muttered hoarsely against her bare shoulder.

"You never asked me," came her quiet response. "The subject of my virginity simply did not come up in the conversation."

"If I had known, I swear to you I never would have done this."

Jennifer touched his rough cheek. "I'm glad you did, Seth. I wanted you to make love to me." It was an honest, sincere confession. After the startling intimacy the two of them had just shared, it was inconceivable to Jennifer to withhold any part of herself from this wonderful man. She snuggled closer to him.

"Jennifer," he pleaded, "we can't let this happen again."

"Why not?" She looked at him in alarm. "Didn't you like it when we—"

Seth pressed a gentle finger to her lips. "Do you even have to ask such a question? It was the most wonderfully exquisite experience I have ever known." He paused painfully. "But it was *wrong*. I had no idea you were such an innocent, and men are supposed to have a code about things like that."

"In what century?"

"Would you listen to me, honey? What we did tonight, it never should have happened. Don't you understand?"

"No." The word was dragged out from between tight lips.

With a regretful sigh, Seth cupped her flushed face in his hands. "You see, I thought—" He stopped and took a breath. "I was sure that Kevin Stern and you—"

Jennifer lowered her lashes. "We were only eighteen years old, Seth."

"But in your generation, everybody is liberated at a far younger age, especially in a fast-lane town like Los Angeles. Naturally, I assumed—"

"You assumed wrong. Kevin had a rigid upbringing. He was determined to wait until we . . . were married."

"But all these years," Seth persisted. "There was never anyone—"

"I'm really tired of this. Do we have to discuss it any longer?" Her brow grew tense. "What's the big deal about being a virgin? Does it make me some kind of freak?''

"No, of course not!''

Jennifer ran a tense hand through her tousled blond mane. "Then why are you acting like this? After everything you said to me, after everything we did, why do you want to push me away?'' Her voice was low. It touched Seth in a way nothing else could have. She sounded so hurt, so vulnerable. It made him feel like the worst kind of monster.

"What can I do to make you understand?'' He shook his head. "You waited so very long to give yourself to a man. It should have been to someone you loved.''

His words were like a knife through her heart. *But I did save myself for someone I love. That someone is you, Seth Garrison.* She wanted to cry from the agonizing unfairness of it all.

He held her in his arms for the rest of the night, but even though warm lips brushed Jennifer's forehead and soothing hands stroked her neck and hair, the actions were those of a chaste lover. His arms soothed and comforted her, but they did not attempt to arouse. In the light of morning, she could see that the sparkle had disappeared from his silver-blue eyes. His expression as he looked at Jennifer was listless, almost somber. Before he left to shower and dress, he drew her back into his powerful embrace one last time. "I know you don't understand this, Jennifer. I know you probably think I'm the lowest kind of character for making love to you and then walking away. But I *have* to walk away from you now, honey. If I don't, I'll go crazy. There's only so much I can take."

"But we're married." Jennifer stared blindly past him at some unseen spot on the wall. "Why can't things go on the way they were?"

"Because—" his hands dropped to his sides sharply "—things can never be the way they were. Not ever again. How can I even look at you without remembering how it was when we made love? How can I live in the same house with you without wanting it to happen again and again?"

"I'm sorry you find that such a repulsive prospect," Jennifer declared chillingly. So much for the idea that seduction would bring a man's heart closer to a woman. She had only succeeded in driving Seth farther away. It was quite obvious that he desired her, but that desire had not the remotest connection to love. He could tremble with excitement in her embrace and take pleasure in the lovemaking act itself, but anything more serious frightened him. The mere fact of her virginity had presented a major stumbling block to his male ego. As long as he had thought she was experienced, there were no stakes. He had felt comfortable in a casual relationship. Jennifer pressed her lips together tightly. That was how men in the eighties were, so many of her girlfriends had warned her. They wanted a woman who was willing to have a good time with no demands and no strings. Instead of seeing her innocence as a prize to be treasured, as a flower in bud to nurture slowly, Seth was acting like a guilty teenager who had just been caught shoplifting.

What an incredibly painful blow to her ego! Jennifer shook her head in disappointment. It was obvious, also, that Seth Garrison was not the man she had thought he was. Oh, certainly, he had fulfilled all her dreams as a tender, infinitely patient lover, but that had been *before* he had discovered her secret. How could she possibly have been so wrong about a person? What had happened to that so-called unerring instinct of hers, anyway?

"Repulsive? Is that what you think?" Seth ground out sharply. "It's all I can do just to keep my hands off of you."

She drew a breath. "At this point I don't particularly care about the problems you're having fighting your baser instincts. You ruined something wonderful for me last night, something that you could have made beautiful and happy."

"For the love of heaven, don't turn the knife!" With an expression of utter misery on his gaunt face, he stalked out of the room and down the hall.

As soon as Seth left the house for his office, Jennifer began repacking her suitcases and putting her books back into boxes. She had every intention of being long gone before Seth returned that evening. There were a number of places where she could stay temporarily. There was always Anita's beach house in

Malibu. Jennifer knew she was always welcome there. She was about to load the first of several boxes into the trunk of her Mustang when sadness overwhelmed her. She felt engulfed by an enormous black cloud. Was this what falling in love could do to a person, she wondered, wiping a stray tear from her cheek. She had been so wise not to have followed Anita's advice to tell Seth about her true feelings. Then his rejection of her would have been complete.

Bitterly Jennifer lifted the first carton into the trunk, and then the second. As she lifted up the third, she somehow lost her grip, and the box went crashing to the concrete floor of the garage, with books tumbling out, spilling everywhere. Suddenly all she wanted to do was weep.

But it wasn't as if she were a child. She had experienced grief and disillusionment before. And she knew that somehow she would be able to summon up the courage to face the pain again and try to get on with her life.

The last thing Jennifer wanted to do was hang around there and feel sorry for herself. With the car keys dangling from her pocket, she decided impulsively to just take off for a while. At first she didn't know where she was going, but the car gradually proved to have a mind of its own. Jennifer found herself driving up a narrow, curving road in Bel Air and turning into a familiar cul-de-sac where she could see the outline of the Ramsey home from behind the trees. She sat and just watched for a while, the site of her happy childhood times filling her aching heart with a warm, nostalgic glow.

Jennifer could almost hear her father's voice, dictatorial but gentle, telling her why she couldn't wear high heels until she was at least nine years old. She suppressed a bittersweet smile. In three months—less, actually—the estate would be her home again. Charlotte would be sent packing once and for all. Up until this morning, Seth had been a part of her new fantasy, the dream of them living together at the rambling Bel Air estate. Even raising a family of their own. She had thought of what a daughter of her own would think of Jennifer's childhood room, with its toys, dolls and picture books still resting neatly on the shelves. If there was a son, would he look like Seth, with that same glossy dark hair and those intense blue eyes?

All at once those previously happy thoughts became a source of bitter pain. There would never be a family with Seth. It had all been an illusion. Jennifer was about to put her car back into gear and get away from there that minute, but almost as if nightmares truly *did* have bad endings, a familiar voice intruded shrilly on her thoughts.

"Well, look who's come to gloat!"

Jennifer's heart sank. Not now, of all times. All she needed at this moment was a confrontation with the Wicked Witch of the West Coast, as Anita had once caustically dubbed Charlotte DeLeon Ramsey. "What a delightful surprise, running into you like this,

Charlotte,'' she muttered. "Too bad the Mustang wasn't going sixty at the time.''

Charlotte didn't reply for a moment. That afternoon she looked harshly beautiful, green mascara accentuating her world-famous eyes and her signature windswept hair tumbling over her shoulders in impeccably choreographed disarray. Her silver workout suit showed off her stupendously youthful figure to absolute perfection. But in the ruthless midday sun, the telltale signs of age were starkly apparent.

"I assure you, Miss Princess of Bel Air, that I have absolutely no intention of vacating *my* home without a fight.'' She leaned arrogantly against the expensive French ten-speed bicycle that she rode every single day. It was the mainstay of her world-famous exercise regimen. "I'm not surrendering this place to you or anybody after the three-month deadline. I live here and I'm going to stay here.''

"Dream on, Charlotte.''

Suddenly it became clear to the woman that her usual intimidation tactics were not as chillingly effective as usual, and that seemed to annoy her even more. "It might interest you to know that I've got some high-powered legal talent in my own corner.''

"Oh, I'm really worried!'' Jennifer shook her head in mild irritation. Growing up in Los Angeles, she had met many film stars over the years. Some were rather modest and easygoing, and others were egotistical and genuinely unpleasant. Her former stepmother fell into the latter category, possessing a nature that, aside from being self-centered and vicious, was also child-ish and insecure.

"Have you done the deed with your four-eyed bridegroom yet?"

A chill swept over Jennifer. She steadfastly refused to become embroiled in a discussion about Seth, par-ticularly after the events of last night. In fact, the only reason she hadn't ignored Charlotte completely and driven away was that, considering her present mood, a nasty little argument with the woman served as a re-lease for her emotions. "That's a crude comment even for someone as low-class as you, Charlotte," she re-torted.

"I do believe the little bride is actually *blushing*. Well, my, my, what a curious development this is." The woman had an uncanny ability to sense a per-son's weaknesses and then go for the jugular. Almost like a bird of prey.

"You don't know what you're talking about, as usual." Jennifer's denial was completely unconvinc-ing.

"Quite a clever operator, that Seth Garrison, un-der his mild-mannered disguise, wouldn't you agree?"

"I don't know what you're talking about."

"Don't play dumb with me. You think I don't know what's up his sleeve?" Charlotte's lips compressed in a thin, ugly line. "Two years ago he's out of Ramsey Enterprises on his ear. And now, with Oliver gone, he waltzes back in like he owns the place." She gave a disgusted cough. "Chairman of the board! What a complete surprise!"

"Not that it's any of your business, but I *asked* him to return to the company. It wasn't his idea at all."

Charlotte laughed shrilly. "That's what you think. I can just imagine the way he sweet-talked you into having everything come out exactly the way he planned."

"This has gone far enough." Jennifer turned on the engine and thrust the Mustang angrily into gear.

"That's right, run away!" Charlotte shouted over the roar of the motor. "But when you get home, why don't you ask Mr. Seth Garrison why he had to leave Ramsey Enterprises in the first place?" She leaned furiously over the handlebars of the racing bike. "Ask your wonderful straight arrow of a husband why he was out of the company all of a sudden! I doubt he'll even tell you the truth! But *I* will! Oliver fired him, that's why! He kicked him right out on his Ivy League behind!"

Jennifer screeched down the road with Charlotte's startling words still ringing in her ears. Of course, she didn't believe anything that nasty woman told her. Charlotte would lie about anything or anybody if it could get her what she wanted. Still shaken, though, Jennifer slowed the car down and drove home at a snail's pace. Much to her astonishment, Seth's car was already in the garage when she pulled into her space. Oh, no. She had been hoping to avoid a confronta-

was doing you a favor by pushing you away." He sighed. "You're so beautiful, so full of life. You deserve someone who can make you happy."

She eyed him steadily. "*You* make me happy."

"Oh, God, don't make it harder than it is to do the right thing." Seth almost choked. "Last night, when we made love, I didn't even use any protection. What if I had made you pregnant?" There was a long silence. "I don't even know that you're *not*, do I?"

Jennifer swallowed. "It's no longer any of your business."

"If there's any possibility of your having my baby, you can damn well better believe it's my business!" His jaw tensed. "Let me make this perfectly clear, Jennifer. Any child of ours is going to have a home with a mother *and* a father."

"I refuse to discuss this any further. If I'm pregnant, whether or not I choose to bring up the child alone is my own affair."

"Not if we're talking about a child of *ours*," came the thick retort.

"A child deserves to grow up in a happy home, where its parents love each other." She paused painfully. "In our case that wouldn't be true."

"Oh, it would be half-true, honey."

"What does that mean?"

His eyes glittered strangely. "What can I tell you that you don't already know? Do I have to wear my heart on my sleeve for you?"

A crystalline light of hope sparked inside Jennifer's heart. "I'm not sure what you're telling me—"

He groaned. "I love you, Jennifer. Everybody in the entire world must have seen it but you."

"You *love* me?"

"Don't make it worse, all right? I'm sure this makes things awkward for you, but I can't help the way I feel . . . the way I've always felt about you since you were sixteen." He turned his head away in embarrassment. "There, I've said it. I've made an absolute jerk out of myself!"

"You're in love with me?" she repeated dumbly.

"Why the hell *else* would I marry you?"

"According to Charlotte, it was the one way to get yourself back into Ramsey Enterprises."

"And you actually believed that redheaded shrew?"

"I'd never believe anything she said, Seth. She even tried to tell me that you left the corporation because Dad fired you."

His face was taut. "That happens to be partially true."

"What? I can't believe my father would ever do such a thing! You were his most trusted friend!"

"You're going to find out sooner or later," he said with a sigh. "But to make it brief, when Charlotte first married your father, she liked to be extra-friendly with any man who just happened to be around. She considered me a challenge because I didn't find her particularly appealing. She made a direct overture to me, and I turned it down. So she went straight to Oliver and told him I had tried to, as she put it, 'make time' with her. She's a wonderful actress, as you well know. She had Oliver convinced that I was trying to steal his loving little wife away from him."

"I can't believe my father swallowed her lies! How could anyone be so blind?"

Seth stared at her intently. "Many people are blind, Jennifer. In any case, your father was shocked that I would try to betray him. He fired me on the spot. He even had me tossed off the grounds of the estate before I could say a single word in my own defense. But later he happened to see Charlotte playing her little games with the man who came to clean the swimming pool. He found me, apologized profusely and asked me to come back. But I couldn't go back there. Charlotte drove me away the same way she did you." He sighed. "I guess your father always knew but just couldn't admit to making such a major mistake. It was that incredible pride of his. Pride can be a dangerous thing, don't you agree?"

Jennifer's face flushed. "I agree," she murmured softly. "If it hadn't been for my foolish Ramsey pride, I would have told you long ago how I—"

He quirked an eyebrow. "How you *what*?"

Her lower lip trembled. This was so hard for her to say, even though she now possessed the thrilling knowledge that Seth loved her. "You were wrong about my feelings for you, Seth. You misjudged me."

"What do you mean?"

"How dense can a man be? After you rant and rave about my being an innocent virgin, and how could I sleep with you instead of holding out for a man I—"

A strange light glimmered a silver-blue. "Finish that sentence, Jennifer."

"What makes you think that I *didn't* hold out for the man I loved?"

He swallowed in disbelief. "I'm imagining this, right? You aren't really telling me what I think you are—"

"I love you." The words came out so simply, so easily now.

"You love me?" Seth was absolutely thunderstruck. "But how could you love me, Jennifer? You're so beautiful, you could have any man you want!"

"I have him, don't I?" She gazed at him shyly.

"Oh, yes, honey." His arms enclosed her in utter happiness. "You have him for as long as you want him."

"Does forever sound all right to you?"

"It's a good start." Seth drew her farther down the hall, into the guest bedroom. "It occurs to me, though, that for an old married couple, we haven't had much of a honeymoon." He took her hand and led her over to the bed. "What would you say to continuing where we left off last night, darling?"

"I'd second the motion," Jennifer agreed shakily as he pressed her down onto the mattress with infinite tenderness. "Ouch!"

"What on earth—" Seth lifted her up, concerned. There, lying on the bed was a hard rectangular object. "Oh, I had forgotten about that," he said sheepishly, handing the package to her. "It's a present I picked up for you this morning, after I had time to think about us."

She unwrapped the package in bewilderment. "What is it?"

"Something I saw in the window of a shop that reminded me of *you*," he teased laughingly.

It was a book. Very old, very rare and very valuable. "I don't believe it," Jennifer cried, hugging him in excitement. It was a leather-bound first edition of *The Sketch Book* by Washington Irving. "I've always wanted an original of this. Did you know it was my favorite book of all time?"

He twisted his lips. "I had a vague idea."

She set it down reverently on the dresser and came back to the bed. "Such a marvelous, delightful gift, Seth. How do I ever begin to thank you?"

He stared at her with that sparkle of silver-blue and drew her down to the pillows with him. "I can think of the perfect way, sweetheart," he said huskily.

*   *   *   *   *

Keepsake

ATTRACTIVE, SPACE SAVING BOOK RACK

Display your most prized novels on this handsome and sturdy book rack. The hand-rubbed walnut finish will blend into your library decor with quiet elegance, providing a practical organizer for your favorite hard-or soft-covered books.

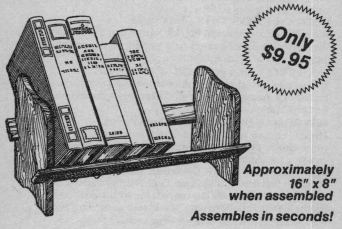

Only $9.95

Approximately 16" x 8" when assembled

Assembles in seconds!

To order, rush your name, address and zip code, along with a check or money order for $10.70* ($9.95 plus 75¢ postage and handling) payable to *Silhouette Books*.

Silhouette Books
Book Rack Offer
901 Fuhrmann Blvd.
P.O. Box 1396
Buffalo, NY 14269-1396

Offer not available in Canada.

*New York and Iowa residents add appropriate sales tax.

BKR-2A

COMING NEXT MONTH

AVAILABLE THIS MONTH